TAKE THE A-TRAIN

Then the yellow Spitfire came tooling down the ramp far too fast, and instead of braking it accelerated and spun across the greasy concrete towards us with a roar from its engine, a scream from the tyres and a cloud of exhaust smoke. The little car skidded broadside, and the edge of the front bumper caught the geezer with the gun on the knee.

I heard bone crack like a bread stick breaking amplified a hundred times, and thought that someone else would be limping for a bit.

The young guy went for something under his jacket. I fumbled the gun off the floor and fired without aiming. I hit him in the meat of his right arm and the parabellum bullet chopped a fountain of flesh and blood and material. He screamed and grabbed at the wound with his left hand.

The Spitfire's engine was howling as Fiona rode the accelerator and jockeyed the clutch. I pulled myself to my feet and jumped over the top of the passenger door, catching my foot a whack that exploded stars in front of my eyes. I held on to the door frame tight and fought back the tears. The tyres laid rubber as we took off . . .

Take the A-Train

Mark Timlin

HEADLINE

First published in 1991
by HEADLINE BOOK PUBLISHING PLC

10 9 8 7 6 5 4 3 2 1

ISBN 0 7472 3699 2

Typeset in 10/11½ pt Mallard
by Colset Private Limited, Singapore

Printed and bound by
Collins Manufacturing, Glasgow

HEADLINE BOOK PUBLISHING PLC
Headline House
79 Great Titchfield Street
London W1P 7FN

This book is for:
HEATHER JEEVES
Who never gives up

RICHARD EVANS
JANE MORPETH
CATHY SCHOFIELD
OLIVER JOHNSON
&
AS ALWAYS,
HMG
WHO FOREVER SAILS WHERE
THE WHITE WATER FLOWS
R.I.P. BABE

1

I was banged up for four months. Four months in traction at St Thomas's, the police hospital, with a thigh bone chipped by a 9 mm short bullet. But only one policeman came and visited me whilst I was there. Socially at least.

At first I was in a room of my own. I think that was more to keep the press away than anything else. Lawyers paid. They paid me too. Mostly to keep me quiet. I'd been working on a case involving two sisters from a very wealthy family. They weren't sisters really, but that's another story. It had all ended rather messily at a building site in Hammersmith. One of the sisters was in an exclusive nursing home. Which is a polite way of saying she was bouncing her head off rubber walls at the cost of a grand a day in an upmarket mental hospital when she should have been in Broadmoor. But money talks louder than justice. The other had moved to Nassau, Bahamas and was permanently incommunicado. I was still in South London and the firm of legal eagles retained by the family had sent me a cheque of such gross proportions, with so many noughts on the end, that it was almost an embarrassment to deposit it at my bank. Almost but not quite. With the cheque came a letter asking me politely to forget the whole incident.

What incident?

After a month, everyone had forgotten who I was and the lawyers stopped paying, so I paid myself. I had the dough and it was a small price for privacy.

I'd had a lot of visitors, considering. Considering I was in a lot of pain from a busted-up leg that just refused to heal. Considering also that my temper was short and my bad moods were long, it was amazing that anyone at all came to visit, a second time at least. My mother came up a few times, and my ex-wife and daughter. My daughter was good, my ex-wife not so. She was large with child, huge in fact. The child wasn't mine. Maybe that was one reason for my bad temper, maybe not. My ex-wife was due any time and loving every minute. I don't think my daughter was quite so pleased. She brought me fruit gums. My daughter, that is.

I was visited by other friends too. Wanda the Cat Woman called in during the first week with a wine cooler stuffed with bottles of imported lager. She looked as luscious as ever, blonde, with a Brixton tan and a load of questions I wasn't about to answer. She asked me if she could do anything for me.

There are a million answers to that; someday I'll write them all down. I asked her to check out my flat and empty the fridge as I knew I was going to be in for a long stay. I gave her my keys and she told me she would. Finally I asked her to keep looking after my cat. She told me she would have done anyway. After she went I drank too much lager and got in a row with my consultant. I told him to go fuck himself, even offered him a lager bottle with

2

which to do it. From then on I got treated by a regular doctor. I didn't mind. The regular doctor was female and had warmer hands.

An old girl friend called Teresa dropped in from time to time but she was living down in Bristol so it wasn't easy for her. Everyone brought something. That was my rule. If they wanted to come up to the tenth floor and watch afternoon TV, then they brought something for me. Shit, it was me that had to sit out the other twenty-two hours of the day when the visitors had split.

Charlie, the mechanic who looks after my cars, came in the second week I was there. He brought me some detective novels. Pretty good they were too. He thought I could maybe get a few pointers from them and stop myself ending up in hospital. I told him it could have been worse. I lined them up on the shelf beside my bed and admired their brightly coloured covers.

Des, who runs a bar in Covent Garden, popped in often during his quiet time in the afternoon and always brought a token bottle. My life fell into a routine pretty quickly. It worked out that I got a visitor every other day throughout the week. I'd sit with my leg up in plaster and traction and talk for a bit and eat grapes, and then I'd get tired and they'd leave. Then I'd run some movies through the little projector in my mind and get depressed and drink the presents I'd been brought and take a pill and sleep perchance to dream . . . aye, there's the rub.

I had a room with a river view. The corner window looked out over South London to Crystal Palace in one direction, and up to Battersea and across the river to Chelsea and beyond in another, and back round to Whitehall in a third. I could look at the river traffic, and the road traffic over Lambeth Bridge, and down Albert Embankment, and soon worked out that if I closed the curtains three-quarters of the way around my bed and kept the curtains at the window open all day, I could get a twenty-four hour movie which beat the one in my head hands down.

So as the summer finished and autumn came I watched the earth turn through that window and the city change from green to brown as the winter began to lock in.

I'd sit in the dawn light, still drunk from last night's sleepers, and listen to hospital radio through impossibly uncomfortable headphones and watch the spires and skyscrapers poke through the mist and wonder if I'd ever be able to walk the cold streets again.

2

On the first Friday in October I was the last to hear that my ex-wife had given birth to a bouncing baby boy a few weeks before, and I realised that another episode of my life was irredeemably over. I also had a brand new visitor. I'd met her twice earlier during that fucked-up summer and if you'd asked me I would have doubted she would even remember my name. She was about five three or four and built so sweet you wanted to eat her underwear. Her name was Fiona. Just that as far as I knew, and she was a model for the tabloids and the wank magazine set.

She pushed open the door to my room around five p.m. when the late afternoon sun was angled across the bed and reflecting through the dark glass of the Moosehead bottle I was holding, making green spectrums across the ceiling. I'd just been given a shave, had my hair washed, and been changed into fresh pyjamas, and even though I say so myself I thought I was looking pretty attractive and she couldn't have picked a better time to call.

'Sharman,' she said from the doorway, 'you look like a big poof.'

She'd been a trifle abrasive when we'd met before so I wasn't as taken aback as I might have been. I maintained my cool and said: 'Oh, it's you. Pull up a toadstool and sit down.' It wasn't great but it was the best I could do at short notice.

She was wearing one of those real short, tube mini dresses made of some clingy material that was so tight you could see where she'd nicked herself shaving her bikini line. It was teamed with dark tights and a Levis jacket that was distressed to the point of tears. Her hair was thick and dark and hung below her shoulders. It caught the sun and absorbed it, then freed it as reluctantly as a lover, and where the sun had touched were highlights of the deepest red.

She let the door close behind her and came over and hitched herself up to sit on the edge of the bed. Her skirt rode up her thighs and I hoped that no medical staff would turn up to take my blood pressure.

'You never called,' she said, fluttering her eyelashes. 'You said you would.'

'I haven't had much time,' I replied, gesturing at my plaster-covered leg. Was she stupid or what?

'So I heard. But I still felt rejected. My maidenly juices began to dry up. It's not often I ask guys to call me.'

'Shit, Fiona,' I said, and I think I fluttered my eyelashes too, 'I didn't know I had such power over women.'

She giggled. Normally I don't like gigglers, but on her a squeaking door would have sounded good. 'You sussed me out, Sharman, and you remembered my name too. You're a real gumshoe, I can tell. Just like on TV. I get off on gory stories and I read all about you in the papers.'

Gumshoe, I ask you!

'So you just popped in to see me? You're lucky they didn't toss you out on your backside,' I said.

'I spoke to a doctor, and he said visitors were good for you. You think too much.'

'Let me guess,' I interrupted. 'In your maidenly way you convinced him that you were a defrocked nun bringing some comforts to my bed of pain.'

'I don't know about the defrocked bit,' she said, 'but I was visiting my dad and I thought I'd come and see you too.'

'Your dad's in hospital?'

'No, he lives in one of the pre-fabs over the road, so I thought I'd look you up.'

'I'm glad you did,' I said. And I really was. So would you have been, believe me.

We kicked some conversational crap around the room as if we were old pals, which we weren't, and even though she was an asset to the surroundings I kept wondering why she'd bothered. When we calmed down, and I started to get used to her thighs, she got to the real nitty gritty. 'So tell me what happened,' she said.

'I'd rather not,' I said back.

'Modest?'

'Hardly. It wasn't one of my finest hours.'

'You did all right, I heard.'

'Not really.'

'I'm sorry,' she said. 'It was a dumb thing to do, coming here. Christ, I feel like a fool now. I think I'd better go.'

'No, don't do that.'

She fiddled around with one of the metal buttons on her jacket and I drank some more beer and the sun moved further down towards the city skyline.

'Is it bad?' she asked.

'What?'

'The leg.'

'No problem,' I said, and gave her the benefit of my best profile as I put the beer bottle on the edge of the wheeled trolley parked at the side of my bed. 'I fuck one of them up every couple of years just to get a month or two in bed.' I rescued the Moosehead and put on a brave, nonchalant face.

I gave her my best profile again and assumed an expression that I hoped teamed steely resolve and boyish charm with just the hint of a sexy twinkle in my eyes. Macho and dependable was the impression I was trying to put over, but my leg chose that moment to give me a reminder that it was still there. I felt a grinding, stabbing agony shoot up my thigh, breathed out sharply, bit down on my lip and spilled the last of the beer down my clean PJs.

'Shit!' I said.

Fiona looked a bit worried and held my arm tightly. 'Shall I call a nurse?'

I squeezed her fingers and the pain went as quickly as it had come. She smelled fresh and sweet. 'No,' I said. 'It's not as bad as it was. I'll be OK.'

'Does that happen often?'

'Not as much as it did, thank God.'

'You've got beer all down yourself,' she said, as if I needed telling.

'There are some clean T-shirts in the cupboard over there. Would you mind?'

I wrestled my wet jacket off and rippled some muscles at her but I don't think she noticed. She hopped off the bed and went over and got me a pale yellow T-shirt from on top of a pile of clean clothes. I slipped it on.

'I brought you something for the pain,' she whispered.

'What?'

She was carrying a black leather shoulder bag just about big enough to take a kitchen sink and all the plumbing. She undid the flap and brought out an old tin cigarette box, so battered that the illustration of a sailor on the lid had worn off in places. I opened it. Inside were six neatly rolled joints. I could smell the dope in the heated air of the room. 'Well, this is a pleasant surprise,' I said.

'Just a little gift.'

I stuck the box into my drawer under some paper tissues then leant over and kissed her on the cheek. Her skin was as soft as a May morning. I could have kissed her all day and half the night. She pushed me away. 'Don't get carried away, Sharman,' she said. 'It's just a bit of dope, not the beginning of a better life.'

'You might be surprised.'

'I'm always prepared to be surprised,' she replied, 'but I'm usually disappointed.'

'You and me both.'

'So surprise me, and offer me a drink.'

I pulled a bottle of Becks from the wine cooler and she wedged the top against the metal bed post and popped the cap off with the palm of her right hand, catching the froth with her left thumb. She picked some scraps of silver paper from around the rim of the bottle and took a long swallow. 'That's great.'

I got myself one of the same and opened it in rather less spectacular fashion, using a bottle opener.

'So what's happening, Fiona?' I asked.

'Usual thing, earning a crust.'

'Keeping in shape?'

'That's for you to say.'

Take my word for it, she was in shape. 'Being good?' I asked.

She shrugged. 'Good-bad, but not evil.'

'Same old grind?' I asked.

'You got it.'

'It's a wonderful life.'

'Fuck me, Sharman, don't tell me you're coming down with a severe case of the moral vapours. I couldn't stand that. After what you've done, showing off my tits is very small potatoes. I may come on like an airhead, but just because I didn't finish my A-levels don't take me for one, OK? I do all right.'

I looked at her in a different light after that little diatribe. And I think I liked her better too. She was right, after all.

She looked a bit miffed for about half a minute and sucked on her bottle like an alcoholic baby, but she soon relented.

'Sorry,' she said. 'I didn't mean to take your head off.'

'My fault,' I said. 'You were right.'

The atmosphere warmed up a bit after that.

'So what do you do around here for laughs?' she asked finally.

'For laughs?' I said. 'Fiona, this is Saint Tommy's, not the WAG Club.'

'Oh, come on, you must do something.'

'Well, the in-crowd gather in the day room and sometimes we organise a big card school.'

'Heavy stakes?'

'Major league. It's been known for a whole box of matches to change hands in a single evening.'

'Anything else?'

'Now and again the anaesthetists have parties, down in the basement. The bloke who plastered my leg up took me down on a trolley.'

'What goes on?'

'The anaesthetists sample their own merchandise. They're well out of order that lot. They're all downer freaks.'

'What happens at these parties then?'

'The one I went to,' I said, 'they poured twelve bottles of Sainsbury's cheap gin into a hip bath and passed ether through it until it turned blue. Mix it with juice to kill the taste and you've got a dynamite cocktail. Makes a Killer Zombie look like choccy milk. I fell off the trolley on the way back and the geezer who was pushing me never noticed.'

'Sounds good. Are they going to have another one soon, I'd like to go?'

'Don't know about that,' I said. 'Anyway, I'm not sure that I can trust the medical staff of this establishment with a girl like you.'

'Why not?'

'The junior doctors don't get enough sleep as it is.'

'Get out of here, Sharman,' she said, but I knew she liked it.

'It's true.'

'Flattery – I knew I was right to come! Shall I come again?'

'I don't know about that,' I said, 'I'm kind of

11

exclusive these days. But you could, I suppose.'

'Your enthusiasm kills me.'

'Infectious, isn't it?'

'So shall I come by and see you again?' she persisted.

'Of course, I was only kidding.' Sure I was. How many other topless models were dropping in? If you'll excuse the expression.

'As long as I don't ask questions about the sisters of mercy.'

I nodded.

'So you do want me to come back?'

'Yeah, I give in. You've got me, Fiona. I'm hooked.'

'It never fails. I just wear this dress and men drop like flies.'

We had another bottle of lager each and after a while she asked me if I was married, and I told her that I wasn't. Then I asked her if she was, and she told me that she wasn't either, and did she look like she was? And I told her that she didn't and asked her if I did, and she told me that I had the look, and bit by bit I told her the whole sorry story and felt better for it.

'So there you go. I'm all alone now with no one to call my own,' I said at the end.

'Tough.' I was glad she didn't give me any fake sympathy.

'Especially on long cold nights,' I said.

'So advertise in the lonely hearts column.'

'I did already.'

'No good, huh, Sharman?'

'The worst. They all wanted to make an honest man out of me,' I said.

'Impossible, I'd say.'

And we smiled at each other, then laughed out loud. I felt good for the first time in months.

'When are you getting out of here?' she asked after a bit.

'I don't know,' I said. 'A month, six weeks maybe.'

'Where do you live?'

'Tulse Hill.'

'How are you getting home?'

I shrugged. 'I don't know,' I said again. 'I'll get a lift somehow, there's plenty of time.'

'I've got a car.'

'Are you volunteering?'

'Maybe.'

'I'll owe you one if you do.'

'One what?'

'Dinner, maybe.'

'A date?'

'If you like.'

'Jesus, Sharman, but you're hard work. I've been angling for a date since I came in here. I thought I was going to have to do handstands to get your attention.'

'Hardly,' I said. 'But I warn you, if you go out with me you have to be careful.'

'Why?'

'It's a walk on the wild side every night with me.'

'Sounds interesting.'

'Stick around and I'll show you.'

'Like when you get your Zimmer frame delivered.'

'The minute it arrives.'

We talked for a bit longer, then she told me that her old man was expecting her for something to eat. All of a sudden I felt lonely for the first time since I'd come into hospital, and in a way resented her for making me so.

'Something wrong?' she asked.

'I'm sorry you're going.'

'I'll be back.'

'Soon?' I asked, and felt pathetic as soon as I said it, but she looked pleased.

'Sure.'

'Great.'

'So get some sleep,' she said.

'Sure,' I said again.

She leant over and kissed me and it went on longer than it should have done. I got a faceful of hair that smelt of Silvikrin and made me think of being out of hospital and all sorts of other things I thought I'd stopped thinking about.

When she pulled away her face was pink, my favourite colour. She jumped down off the bed and got her things together.

'Hey!' I said as she was leaving. She paused in the doorway, holding the handle and sort of half-way out of the room.

'What?'

'Thanks for the visit. I appreciated it, really.'

'My pleasure,' she said, and blew me a kiss with her free hand.

She went out and the door closed behind her and the room wasn't as bright as it had been when she was there.

3

I smoked the joints, and they did help the pain, fleetingly, but that's the way life goes, I've discovered.

Fiona came and visited me a lot after that. I really didn't know what the attraction was, and didn't care much either. Then in the first week of November my consultant deigned to grant me an interview.

He stood over me, his acolytes behind him: the female doctor who'd looked after me, a houseman, a couple of vague students and several nurses with different shades of uniform and shapes of hats. 'We're going to let you out early,' said my consultant. 'We've done all we can here. Stay in bed for three weeks at home then come back and we'll take the plaster off. It's just healing time you need now.'

'And you could use the bed,' I pointed out.

'Of course we can always use an empty bed. It's just a waste of your money staying here. Have you got someone to look after you?'

I shrugged as much as you can in traction. 'I guess.'

'Fine.' He rubbed his perfectly clean and manicured hands together. 'As soon as we've cleared you out, a physio will come up and teach

15

you how to use the crutches, then you're free to leave.'

I interrupted. 'I know about crutches.'

'The physio will have to be convinced.'

I tuned him out and lay back. 'Bring on the physios then.'

Fiona came to visit that evening and I told her I was free to go home.

'Great!' she said. 'Do you still want a lift?'

'Yes, please.'

Wanda had cleaned up and closed down my flat and brought my keys back. I gave them to Fiona and she went off to check the place out and get some food in and put the heating on. She was back within a couple of hours.

'You can't stay there,' she said briskly.

'Why not?' I asked. 'I live there.'

'There are too many stairs for you to get up and down for a start, and there's no bath. You can't be in plaster and use a shower. And if you stay there someone will have to come and look after you, and the place is far too small for two.'

'So?'

'Come and stay at my place. It's got three bedrooms and I can look after you with no bother.'

'Haven't you got anything to do? No work, I mean.'

'Sure, but it's not nine to five. I can fit you in.'

'Sounds good.'

'Unless the lift breaks down.'

'What?'

'I'm on the twenty-seventh floor.'

'How many?'

'Twenty-seven,' she said proudly.

'Where the hell do you live then?'

'Tower block. Top floor, babes, but it's great when you get there.'

'Does the lift break down often?'

'Often enough.'

'And if it does?'

'Piggy back for you, son, but don't worry – I'm sure it'll be all right.'

'Not a good idea. I'd sooner be home.'

'Cooking for yourself and drowning in your own dirt?'

I thought about it for a moment, the advantages and the disadvantages. 'OK, Fiona,' I said. 'You've talked me into it.'

'There goes that old enthusiasm again.'

'Sorry, I was just thinking.'

'Dangerous thing to do, Sharman. Cut it out, will you?'

'I'll try.'

The next morning she picked up my suitcase and an overnight bag and a couple of plastic carriers. You stay in hospital for sixteen weeks and you start to acquire stuff you don't want to leave behind. Clothes, books, all sorts of shit people had brought me and I wasn't about to dump. Fiona was dressed in a thick brown leather jacket with a fur collar over a big sweater that reached halfway down her thighs, and woolly leggings tucked into high-heeled boots. Around her neck she wore a long scarf striped black and white. 'Christ!' she said as I passed her the bags and stuff, 'this lot weighs a ton.'

A couple of nurses had come in to say goodbye. One had brought me my take-away drugs: pain killers, sleepers, etc. I thanked the nurses and

apologised, I hoped sincerely, for any trouble I'd
given them. They were all smiles but I knew they'd
forget about me by shift end. That was OK, I
expected them to. It was the nature of the job.

I used both crutches and pushed myself along
beside Fiona, past the open wards, through into the
waiting area and out to the lifts. It was strange to
be mobile again, even in a limited way; strange to
see people uninterested in my welfare.

We descended in the big lift that smelt of old food
down to the lower ground floor and out to the car
park. 'I'm over there,' said Fiona.

I'd never thought to ask what kind of car she had,
but I guessed as soon as I saw it sitting in its slot. It
was an acid yellow Spitfire – with the roof down.
The weather outside was cold and getting colder.
'You need to put the hood up,' I said.

'There isn't one. It got slashed a month ago and
I haven't had it replaced.'

'What happens when it rains.'

'I get wet.'

'Lovely,' I said. 'I suppose that explains the kit.'

She looked down at herself and giggled. The
giggle still worked and I smiled, against my better
judgement. I was wearing a maroon sweater with
a shawl collar over a pale lemon Oxford cotton
shirt and ancient 501s with the left leg chopped off
to accommodate my cast. I wasn't dressed for the
Arctic.

'I brought a coat for you to wear. It's in the boot.'
She dropped my stuff and opened the boot, pulling
out my blue Crombie and shaking out the creases. 'I
got it from your flat.'

'I can't wear that and use these,' I said petulantly, referring to the crutches. 'Fucking hell, Fiona!'

'Now don't get difficult,' she said. 'I know it's a drag, but it's only a ten-minute drive and the fresh air will do you good. Your face looks like a fish belly.' She cracked up.

I gave her another thin smile and leant the crutches up against the side of the car, put on the coat and thanked Christ for dry weather.

The car was too small for me and the plaster cast, even with the passenger seat way back. Eventually I wedged myself in and gathered the skirts of my coat and the remains of my dignity around myself. With my crutches sticking out of the back seat, we set off.

She drove like I guessed she would, flat out. She pushed the needle of the rev counter into the red in every gear, and the small engine and the tyres protested like hell, but she never let up.

We drove straight to Camberwell. Halfway there she pointed out the three high-rise blocks that stood looming over Kennington Park.

'I live in the nearest one,' she shouted over the roar of the engine and the wind. 'You're in luck. The lifts are working today.' She downshifted and overtook a grey Mercedes on the inside coming up to the lights at Kennington Cross. The transmission clunked in disgust. She turned and looked at me and added, 'At least, they were.'

'Watch the bloody road!' I said.

'Don't worry, you'll be all right.'

I looked through the slipstream and felt my eyes tear from the force and thought how beautiful she looked at that moment, with her face animated and her hair tossed by the wind. 'I hope so,' I yelled. 'Or else I'm camping in the lobby.'

'You wouldn't last five minutes,' she said, and her laugh was ripped away by the wind.

We pulled up in the shadow of the tower block. Fiona dragged my stuff out of the boot and I dragged myself out of the cockpit.

'I'm going to park the car,' she said. 'Won't be long.'

'Where do you leave it?'

'I've rented a garage since I lost the third hood in four months.'

'You were lucky to get one round here.'

'I wore a very short skirt when I went looking,' she said. 'Now the guy who rents it to me wants to be my special friend.'

'I bet he does!'

'Free parking.'

'And?'

'And I'd rather pay double. Wait here. I won't be two minutes.'

She was four but I didn't care. Even under the shadow of that brute of a building it was good to be out in the world again. She came trotting back, chest heaving. Even under all that leather and wool it was quite a sight. 'Come on,' she said, gathered up my stuff and set off. I followed her through the filthy glass doors. The place was graffiti heaven. It was freezing cold and someone had pissed in the corner. It smelt like a zoo. There were a bunch of kids, black and white mixed, huddled together in one corner around a beat box. The volume was turned all the way up and the cheap speakers distorted the sound to mush.

'Damn!' I said.

The kids perked up when we came in. I guessed we made good sport. They started making comments – plenty of 'fucks' and 'cunts' and 'shits', all laced together for maximum offence. There were some mentions of my crippled state. Fiona pulled a face and shook her head when she thought I might say something back. Eventually the lift came. A couple of the kids made as if to join us and keep up the game. It was my turn to shake my head then and slide my right hand down its crutch to make a crude club. The kids were young enough to take the hint, just. Another couple of years and who knows?

The lift doors closed behind us and I relaxed against the wall. There was more graffiti inside. It made the interior of the cage oppressive and tight like a prison cell. It smelled like one too, like the lobby, like a shithouse, and I wondered how this girl managed to live here all the time.

'For God's sake, Fiona!' I said.

'Hard to lets,' she replied. 'I queued for two days and a night on a cold pavement outside the town hall to get this place. I've put too much effort in to let a few little sods like that frighten me away.'

'Not so little.'

'Anyway, it's your fault, you look like a copper. It'll be all right once we get inside the flat.'

'Does that happen often?' I asked.

'No, not really. It's the weather driving them inside. I get some wolf whistles and dirty talk but I ignore it.'

'And what happens if it's more than talk?'

'My dad taught me some moves.'

'Like?'

'Army things, plus a little extra. I told you he was in the SAS, didn't I? I can take care of myself.'

'I hope so,' I said. 'But don't worry, I'm here now.'

'That's a relief,' she said, and I suppose standing there propped up by two bits of metal tube and plastic and rubber I wasn't exactly as reassuring as I might have been.

The lift shuddered upwards. It seemed to take forever on its journey. The floor indicator was history. It had been ripped away from above the door and just two bits of bent wire and some battered numerals were left. A couple of times the lift faltered and seemed to be on the verge of giving up altogether and I thought sourly that I might spend most of my first day of freedom being jacked up or down a lift shaft by the fire brigade. Fiona stayed cool so I assumed the lift's behaviour was nothing out of the ordinary.

After what seemed like an hour we ground to a halt and the doors slid open with a screech of protest. We walked, or in my case limped, on to a half clean hallway with a door at each end and another jammed half open, leading on to the stairwell. Fiona turned left and dumped my bags in front of her flat. The door was painted sick green and held a security peeper and three key holes. It was battered-looking and someone had tried to get a blunt instrument between door and jamb. The scars on the paint looked fresh.

'My dad fitted a metal door,' she explained proudly. 'And the locks and the dead bolt. The spy hole and the letter box can be locked from the inside.'

'He's handy, your dad.'

'You'd better believe it, and my brother too. So be careful, Sharman, or they'll come and get you.'

'I never argue with the military.'

She juggled a set of keys from the pocket of her leather jacket and took an age to open up. What she'd do if anyone came after her whilst she was trying to get through that bank of security I didn't ask, but I wasn't happy. I thought I might talk to her father or her brother about it.

The front door opened on to a short hallway with a door each side. At the end was a steep open staircase. 'It's a maisonette,' she said. 'Kitchen on the left.' She threw open the door and I registered a clean white kitchen with a blind pulled down over the window. 'Living room on the right, but it gets a bit noisy sometimes at night. The people downstairs are party animals, so I don't use it. It's all right – upstairs you can't hear a thing.' She opened that door and let it bounce back on itself and I had a glimpse of a huge empty room with dark curtains drawn across a wall-width window. 'Can you manage the stairs?' she asked. 'Here, give me your coat.'

I leant the crutches against the wall, shrugged out of the Crombie and handed it to her. I fitted my arms back into the crutches and heaved myself up a dozen stairs and into a hall that turned back on itself at the top.

'Bathroom,' she indicated.

It was a medium-sized room with towels folded neatly over a rail and only one pair of tights hanging over the bath. She pulled them down, felt them for dampness, seemed satisfied and brought them with her. 'I cleaned up for you. It was in a bit of a mess.'

I backed out awkwardly.

'Bedroom one,' she said. 'I use this as a living room.' Another door opened on to a darkened room, curtains closed again. It was furnished with a two-piece suite that looked expensive, and a TV and video on a trolley with wheels.

'Bedroom two.' Another dark, empty room. No furniture, especially no bed.

'Bedroom three.' I was getting tired as she showed me a huge room with a built-in wardrobe and dressing table, both dominated by a massive bed – and I mean massive, fully eight feet by six. Even though I estimated that the room was twenty feet square, with a high ceiling, it was dominated by the bed. It had a padded headboard and no baseboard and was covered by a colourful duvet. Fiona ignored it.

'This is the biggest window,' she said, and walked in and drew back the curtains.

The wall seemed to be all glass. Outside was a balcony, maybe three or four feet deep, and after that nothing until the hard concrete twenty-seven storeys down. I couldn't believe that anyone would step out on to that exposed ledge. Beyond the balcony was the view. I've never seen one like it. I looked out over the park to the Elephant and the river beyond, and counted seven or eight bridges. I could see right over the City of London to the hills beyond. The city appeared to fill the room. We seemed to be floating over the rooftops as if in a dream.

The place was silent until Fiona slipped a catch and slid the window open. I could hear the city then, the noise of eight million people and their cars, and the wind whistling around the roof like a mad thing, even though down below in the street the day had seemed quite still.

'Christ!' I said. 'That *is* a view.'

'I closed all the curtains in the flat so I could surprise you,' she said. 'But just you wait for night time.'

'Draughty up here,' I said.

'This is nothing. There's a three-foot sway when it gets really blowy.'

I turned away from the window. It was too much to take in at one go. 'By the way, where am I sleeping?'

'Don't be coy, Sharman,' she said. 'You're in here with me. I'm as horny as hell, and I've been waiting for this for weeks.'

'But my leg,' I said.

'Don't worry about that, just leave it to me. I guarantee absolutely no pain.' I gave her a look. 'Well, maybe just a little.'

4

'Do you want a joint to get you in the mood?' Fiona asked. This was 9 a.m. remember. 'Or a drink? Oh, Christ, I'm sorry, do you want something to eat?' She'd obviously remembered that our relationship was supposed to be nurse/patient rather than dominatrix/sex slave, although I could handle that.

'No food,' I said. 'I've just eaten a Saint Thomas's egg and I think it's digesting me. But I could use a beer.'

'No problem. Get into bed,' said Fiona.

'Remember I'm ill,' I said.

'Sure, I mean to rest. Christ, I'm nervous all of a sudden.'

'Don't spill the beer.'

'No, I won't, now get into bed.' She stood for a minute and I sort of leaned awkwardly against the wardrobe, waiting for her to go. 'Oh, sorry,' she said. 'I'll leave you to get undressed.'

'Been doing it for years, all by myself,' I said with forced heartiness.

She went out of the room and I wondered what I'd let myself in for, then shrugged and sat on the side of the bed. I piled my clothes at the end of the bed. I didn't want to get into wardrobe-space wars for a bit.

I got in between the sheets, dragging my leg behind me. The bed was big and comfortable and the sheets were soft and freshly laundered and smelt of woman, all in all as different from a hospital crib as could be. Like an idiot I got a hard on straight away. I snuggled down and looked straight out over London. Fiona had positioned the bed for maximum visual overload.

She came back with two cans of Bud, freezing from the refrigerator. 'What do you want?' she asked as I chugged at one. I must have looked puzzled across the top of the can. 'Music, TV, a film? I've got loads of tapes.'

'Whatever,' I said, concentrating on the beer.

She went off again and came back, pushing the TV and video on its trolley. She plugged everything in and pushed a button on the set. 'Here's the remote,' she said, throwing me the little, black plastic box. 'It works the TV and the video. Figure it out if you can. It took me months.'

I pressed buttons and got two soaps, Ceefax and *Rainbow*. I turned the volume down on Zippy. Whatever happened to *Button Moon*? I used to watch it with my daughter. All of a sudden I felt like crying. I was homesick for the hospital.

Fiona saw I was having some kind of withdrawal and rolled a joint of pungent Thai grass. We smoked it, listening to *Killing Joke* on the stereo.

I lay there for nearly an hour as Fiona changed the records and *Rainbow* turned into *The Gummi Bears* and a few flakes of snow dislodged themselves from the November sky and drifted past the window. She had loaded the joint until it nearly capsized and I felt no pain.

I must have fallen asleep and woke up with a start. Fiona was still sitting at the foot of the bed. The news was on TV and there was a guitar band that I didn't recognise creeping softly through the stereo. 'What's the time?' I asked.

'Twelve. Are you hungry yet?'

'No.'

Silence.

'I have to talk to you,' she said.

'What about?'

'Sex.'

'I had a blood test,' I said. 'Recently, if that's what you're worried about.'

'No, it's not that. It's about when we first met.'

'Yes?'

'I wanted to shock you.'

'You did, a bit.'

'God, I'm embarrassed.'

'Why?'

'I showed you my tits.'

She had, in public, at a party.

I smiled. 'So you did,' I said. 'And they were all right. More than all right, as it happens. But what's the big deal? You do it every day.'

'That's different. That's business. I liked you – I mean, I like you.'

'I like you too.'

'No, I mean I *really* liked you, straight away. That doesn't often happen to me.'

'I warned you about my fatal charm.'

'Don't joke, Sharman.'

'Sorry.'

'You see, I've only had two lovers before and one was a mistake.'

'Fifty per cent, that's good. I wish my average was as high.'

'No,' she said wistfully, 'they were both mistakes really.'

'That's more realistic,' I said. 'Nil percent. That's about right.'

'I thought I loved him, the first one. I thought it was really love.'

'Don't we all?'

'Don't be so cynical.'

'You're confusing cynicism with telling the truth. Anything else is fairytales, like *The Gummi Bears*.'

'I hate to hear you talk like that, as if you really believe it.'

'I do,' I said.

'We were going to get married.'

'A lucky escape.'

'Then I rebounded on to a real yuk.'

'And now?'

'Now you.'

'Maybe I'm another real yuk.'

'I hope not.'

'So do I.'

'Shall I roll another joint?' she asked.

'In a minute. I need to go to the loo.'

'I'm no good as a nurse, I'm afraid.'

'You're great.'

'I got you a bottle. You know, to piss in.'

'Are you serious?' I asked.

'Yes, I stole one from the hospital. Was that terrible?'

'No, I paid them enough. But with a little help, I think I can manage to get to the bathroom.'

So I went to the toilet by myself. Big deal, the average three-year-old can do it too, but I was proud of myself nevertheless. When I got back to the bedroom Fiona had rolled another joint. We smoked it and drank more beer. I got hungry and she made steak sandwiches, heavy on the mustard. We watched a tape of *The Big Heat*. The afternoon went and the night arrived and the lights came on all over London. We didn't turn the lights on in the bedroom. She found her one jazz album and we played *Take The A-Train* by Duke Ellington and watched the rush hour trains below. After the music finished Fiona undressed and came to bed with me. We cuddled and watched from our silent eyrie.

Eventually she rolled over and faced me in the dim light that came from outside. 'How long since you had a fuck, Sharman?'

'Months.' I didn't want to think about it.

'None of those pretty nurses help you out? I got some dirty looks when I started to come round.'

I held her away from me and said, 'They have a policy at the hospital – pure food and pure staff. No, Fiona, none of the pretty nurses helped me out. One called me a prick one night though.'

'Why?'

'I called her "Nursey, Nursey". Apparently nurses don't like that sort of thing. I was drunk.'

'I'd've called you a prick too.'

'Thanks, Fiona.'

'Don't mention it. You want to fuck now?'

'I don't know.'

'That thing's pretty hard down there.'

'What?' I asked, surprised.

'Your plaster cast, what did you think I meant?'

I laughed. 'You're good, Fiona, you know that?'

'Kiss me then.'

So I did. She tasted like a flower of romance, sweet and buttery, and then I had two hard things down there and she went down on both of them. I followed her with my hands until she went too far, and then I just lay on my back looking up at the ceiling. She pushed the covers back and rubbed herself on my cast until she came with a loud exhalation of breath and then she mounted me. We both called out, but not to each other. I reached one hand out and touched her belly. It was hot like fire and I kept my hand there whilst I caressed her leg with the other.

Her skin was as slick and smooth as warm soap. I ran my hand up her thigh, over her waist, up her side, and cupped her breast and rubbed her nipple with my thumb. She moaned and arched over me, then rolled over dragging me with her. I felt a stab under my plaster and came with the pain.

'Oh, you fucker,' she said. 'I wanted another one.'

'Sorry.'

She pulled away from me and grabbed a handful of tissues from the box on the table by the bed to dry herself. 'Christ, Sharman,' she said, 'but you're a sloppy bastard.'

She threw the tissues at me and they hit me wetly in the face.

'Cheers,' I said.

That was one thing I was to learn about Fiona –

there was no after-sex tenderness with her. 'Christ, I've got to eat, eat, eat,' she said.

She grabbed her knickers from the floor, made a face and pulled them on, on the run. She vanished through the bedroom door and I heard clattering and slamming from the kitchen downstairs. She came back with a trayful of food. 'My fridge is a tip,' she said, dumping the tray on the bed. She'd brought enough for five. There was cold pizza, prawns, cheese, salad, biscuits, a bottle of wine, plates, cutlery, napkins, the works.

She got back into bed and switched on the TV. We watched the news again as we ate, then lots of programmes I can't remember. I do remember that we drank the wine, then another bottle, and got high again and made love a couple more times before we fell asleep.

5

For the next three weeks I lay there, in that bed in the sky, and Fiona looked after me, in more ways than one. I was screwed, blewed and tattooed, and loved every minute. I discovered that she had a dirty mind, very dirty, and she had lots of fantasies and liked to work them out and hear them described in graphic detail afterwards.

And then I went back to the hospital and the plaster caster took a wicked-looking electric buzz saw and slid it through my plaster as smoothly as a hot knife through ice cream. I only felt a slight tickle once, although I must admit to a certain tightening of my rear end as he did the job. My left leg looked like a dead stick covered in layers of old newspaper. Dried skin peeled and fell from it like autumn leaves. I limped up to see my consultant and he declared me ready for physiotherapy. He presented me with an elastic sock and a walking stick and I never saw him again. At least I got to wear trousers with two legs again, and a pair of socks and a pair of shoes.

The physios were sadists to a man, or woman to be more accurate. Pretty yes, neat yes, present-able yes, sexy yes, but sadists one and all. They ran me ragged for weeks but gradually my leg got

35

better, bit by bit, although I couldn't bear to look at the livid scars that the operations had left.

When the plaster came off and the physio began, I moved back to my own flat, not on a permanent basis, you understand, but every other night or so.

Ten days or so before Christmas, a Thursday it was, I finished my hour with a particularly delectable but particularly vicious physio who just loved to see me suffer and sweat on the parallel bars. I limped out of the 'In' door of Casualty, under the concrete awning and into a fine spray of thin, cold rain. I walked across the paved walking area, down the few steps to the main road. The rain was insinuating itself down my neck so I pulled up the collar of my overcoat as I went, rapping myself painfully on the knee with the end of my stick as I did so. I swore and looked right on the off chance that a cab might be heading towards Westminster Bridge with its amber light glowing. In that kind of weather I would have had more chance of seeing a flock of sheep or a group of Djerba dancers.

As I reached the pavement a dark blue stretch Lincoln Town Car that had been parked opposite pulled through a hole in the traffic heading east and glided to a halt at the kerb beside me. I broke step. How did I know it was for me? I didn't. How did I know that behind the mirrored glass there weren't half a dozen guns pointed at me? I didn't.

The car sat for ten seconds, engine running, a faint grey exhaust cloud chugging from the rear pipe made visible by the freezing air outside. I felt panic-stricken for a heart beat, then relaxed. If the occupants of the car wanted me, they had me cold. The kerbside front window hummed down and I was looking into a pair of dark pupils set like buttons in a slightly yellow white of eye. The face behind the eyes had ebony skin topped with a bush of nappy black hair. The owner wore an expensive brown leather jacket, collar turned up all the way to his chin.

'Mr Sharman, I presume,' he said in one of those nice friendly West Indian accents that could charm the briefs off a mother superior. 'So sorry to see you indisposed.' I shrugged and tapped my cane against my shoe. 'I wonder if you have some time to spare?' the black man went on.

I smiled a tight smile, but said nothing.

'Mr Watkins would like to see you.'

Emerald.

'Where is he?' I asked, as I stood on the rain-swept pavement and got wetter.

'Not far away.'

'Once upon a time he'd have asked me himself. Friends do that.'

'He sends his apologies. He hopes you will understand. Business duties he could not avoid.'

'And you are?' I asked.

'My name is Lupus. I work for Mr Watkins.'

'Since when?'

'Quite recently. He found that there was too much for one man to handle.'

'So you're the boy.'

The black man gritted his teeth. I could almost hear them grinding together and I didn't mind so much getting wet.

'Hardly,' he said. 'I am Mr Watkins's personal assistant.'

'How grand. When I first met him, he was doing all the cooking in his place.'

'Not any more.'

I looked along the length of the car as it gleamed in the dull mid-morning light under its coating of fine moisture. 'So I see. Business must be good.'

'Adequate.'

'And Em wants to see me?'

Lupus frowned at the name I gave his employer. 'Mr Watkins, yes.'

'Tell him to give me a bell, he's got the number,' I said, and walked away from the car. There was another black guy leaning against the traffic light standard. He was just leaning, tall and broad in a light showerproof coat. Then he smiled at me and I heard the doors of the car open and looked round and saw two more Brothers getting out of the back of the Lincoln, one each side. The guy who had been leaning non-chalantly waiting for the lights to change was right up close to me now. He frisked me under my arms and around my waist and I stood for it.

'He favours something on the ankle,' one of the others said behind me.

I shook my head. 'I never go to advanced physio-therapy armed. It tends to upset the rhythm of the whole class.'

The guy in the light mac gave me a big smile. 'I trust you,' he whispered. 'Don't disappoint me.'

'I'll try desperately hard not to.'

'Get into the car,' he ordered.

'Make me,' I said, stubborn to the end. You would

have thought that limping around on a stick for weeks would have taught me some kind of a lesson.

He blew through his teeth. 'Don't be stupid,' he said. 'I hate hurting cripples, it ruins my day.'

'I'd regret being the cause of that.'

The car reversed up to where we were standing. 'Count on it,' he said. 'Now get in.'

I did as I was told. I ducked down into the back of the limousine and on to the broad leather seat. I sat in the middle and the guy in the light mac sat next to me. One of the men who had got out of the back of the car sat in the jump seat opposite. The other walked round into the traffic and got in on that side and took the other window seat. The upholstery was so deep that my knees were about level with my eyes. Although there were three of us in the back seat the car was wide enough to allow room for a keg of beer between each of us. Light Mac turned round and put one ankle on his knee. He took my stick and gave it to Jump Seat who studied it carefully.

'No sword,' I said. 'I'm afraid the NHS doesn't run to them.'

Jump Seat pursed his lips but said nothing. Eventually he put the stick on the floor.

The car pulled into traffic and the black glass partition between us and the chauffeur's compartment whirred down. Once again I was looking into the dark eyes of the man sitting beside the driver. 'Hello again,' I said.

He nodded.

'Mens,' the driver said.

I looked through the one-way glass of the back window and saw a squad car behind us. Light

Mac looked at me and put his finger to his lips.

'Relax,' said Lupus. 'Everything is cool.'

And it was. The squad car accelerated and pulled past us and got lost somewhere around Lambeth Palace.

The Lincoln sizzled through the rainy streets across Lambeth Bridge, up through Pimlico and Victoria, across Hyde Park into the Bayswater Road, right at Notting Hill tube and through a maze of grey side streets until the Westway loomed overhead.

The rain got worse as we drove and the loudest sound was the windscreen wipers beating double time to clear the driver's vision. Inside the car, all was quiet and serious. No one spoke or smoked or snapped gum or pulled funny faces. Everyone looked anywhere except at each other.

The driver stopped outside a set of high wooden gates in a high wooden fence. He waited until the street was empty of pedestrians and moving traffic, then leaving the engine running, got out of the car and ran through the rain. He pushed the gates open, ran back, manoeuvred the car through the gates, stopped again and ran back and closed the gates behind us.

I watched through the side window and saw that inside the fence was a landscape as barren and colourless as the surface of the moon. The area was empty except for three sets of huge concrete pillars holding up the motorway and two other parked cars. One was an empty, navy blue three series BMW; the other a black Mercedes saloon with windows as dark as the Lincoln's. Our driver headed slowly towards the two parked cars that sat as still and malevolent as a pair of cockroaches waiting for a crumb of cheese. We slid to a halt beside the Merc.

Light Mac opened the door and stepped out. He leaned back into the car and said to me, 'Come on, let's go.'

I didn't argue. 'Stick,' I said. Jump Seat passed it to me. I climbed awkwardly out of the car and leant hard down on the stick as I followed Light Mac across a crust of packed grey dirt, criss-crossed with tyre tracks that broke under my shoes like old concrete.

It was dark and cold under the motorway, and noisy from the rumble of wheels and engines above us. Long, filthy grey stalactites hung down from underneath the road and dripped brackish water on to the ground. Light Mac walked to the Mercedes and opened one of the back doors. He bent at the waist and looked inside. He said something I couldn't hear, straightened up and beck-oned for me to come closer.

I limped over and he stepped away from the car. I saw a familiar huge figure sitting in the middle of the back seat.

'Join me, Nick,' said an equally familiar voice.

I ducked down and climbed into the car and sat next to Emerald on the leather-upholstered seat. I checked him out. By the looks of the threads he had finally laid his Motown period to rest. The material that covered his ample person was pure Savile Row. It was about as understated as a grand could buy, and just as beautifully cut. His shirt was as soft and white as a dove's feather and you could shave by the shine on his shoes. On his pinky finger was the stone that gave him his nick-name – huge and green and set in enough gold to fill a football team's teeth.

'Nicky,' he said.

'Emerald,' I said back. 'Or should it be Mr Watkins these days? You seem to have come up in the world. A personal assistant even. It's all very smart.'

'I had some luck with an investment a while back. I've expanded since we last met.'

'So I see. The firm's getting bigger, if not more pleasant to deal with. A real black success story.'

Emerald's crew were well known round south London. I'd first bumped into them when I was on the force. Emerald had run drinking and gambling clubs and prostitutes for years. He'd always been good to me and mine, and at the time I'd turned a blind eye to his larkins. We'd cleared all outstanding debts about eighteen months before. I hadn't seen him since, but I still considered that we were friends.

'I wish I'd stayed as I was. I had fewer enemies.'

'You didn't do too bad, as far as I remember.'

'Plenty of friends too, including you.'

'If I'm a friend, why send your boys to kidnap me? A telephone call would have done. You knew I'd come.'

'There was no time.'

'So what's the deal, man? What business brings you to this Godforsaken place?'

'The end of my business.'

'Oh, yeah, how come?'

'There's a warrant out for my arrest.'

'Not the first.'

'No, but this is heavy.'

'Have you been watering the scotch down the club?'

'No, Nick. Possession of controlled drugs with intent to supply.'

There's not much you can say to that. 'Oh yeah?' was the best I could come up with.

'Yeah.'

'What kind of drugs?'

'Cocaine.'

'How much?'

'Half a million quid's worth.'

I looked at him to see if he was serious, and he appeared to be. 'How much?' I asked.

'You heard.'

'For real?'

'For real.'

'You naughty boy, you should be ashamed.'

He sucked sharply through his teeth with an angry sound. 'I've been done up.'

'You would say that.'

'Don't you believe me?'

'Are you telling me?'

'Yes.' He looked at me as if it really mattered what I thought.

'Then I believe you,' I said, and I did. That's what friends are for. 'It doesn't seem to have upset the visuals any. That's a nice suit, and the cars and all.'

'If I'm going down, I'm not going down scruffy,' he said.

'That sounds like you. But where exactly do I fit in?'

'I need help.'

'Don't we all?'

'I'm serious.'

'Get a good brief.'

He sighed. 'Not that kind of help. I need someone in your line of work.'

'I have no line,' I replied. 'I'm convalescing.' I tapped my leg with my stick.

He looked angrily at me. 'Don't fuck around, Nick. I need your help.'

'You want to hire me?'

'Yes.'

'You're crazy.'

'I did the right thing by you not long ago, now do the right thing by me.'

And there it was. As inevitably as night followed day. The catch. The sting. One hand washing the other. But he was right. Emerald had supplied me with a couple of guns when I needed them and had nowhere else to turn. Like I said, I thought all debts had been cleared but obviously I was wrong.

'A favour for a favour?' I asked.

'Something like that.'

'I'm half crippled, Em,' I said. 'As your boy in the raincoat keeps reminding me, and he's right.'

'There's no one better.'

I laughed. 'Don't bullshit a bullshitter, Em,' I said. 'We don't need to go through my references, we're mates. I'll do what I can, you know that. But why me?'

'Because if I want something out of a chicken coop, I don't send in a fox, I send in another chicken.'

'Your analogy is charming, if a little abstruse. Why don't you send it by me one more time, in words of one syllable?'

'All my guys are black,' he explained. 'You're white. You can go where they can't.'

'I'll make sure I add that to my CV,' I said. 'All right, Em, you got me.'

'I knew I could count on you.'

'Tell me the whole sad story,' I said. 'And can you get some heat in here? I'm freezing my arse off.'

Emerald tapped on the glass dividing us from the driver and it rolled down. He told the guy behind the wheel to turn on the heater. The driver started the engine and soon warm air began to seep through the vents in the side of the car and the glass rolled smoothly up again. I cracked the window next to me for ventilation and lit a cigarette as Emerald told me what had happened.

'I still got a few friends in CID,' he said. 'Not so many as before. Things have changed. The Met's trying to clean up its act again. But there's a few favours outstanding. I got a call last night, was told that there were warrants out for all my premises and my home.'

'All your premises?' I interrupted.

'The old club in Clapham, three pubs, a restaurant, and a few other odds and ends.'

'Christ, things *have* changed. Are you sure you're not pushing coke?'

His dark face grew even darker and he gave me a long, vicious look.

'Joke, Em,' I said.

'I'm not in the mood.'

'Fair enough. But one day you must tell me where the money came from.'

'It's no secret, and legal too. Now can I get on? I don't have all day.'

'Sure.'

'I sent some of the boys round to check my places. All's serene. Everything safe. I took my wife to her sister's last night and I stayed there too. The sister's straight. Her and her husband mind their business and go to church Sundays. I mind mine and don't, but family is family. They took us in, no questions. I left Teddy at my place to mind the store.'

'Who?'

'My nephew, the boy in the raincoat.'

'I didn't know you had a nephew.'

'My brother's boy. They live in Southampton. He came to work for me last year.'

'He doesn't have your manners,' I remarked.

'He's feeling stress, but you're right, it's no excuse. I'll see him. Anyway, I've got this lock up. Down Wandsworth Road, under the arches. By the station, you know.'

I nodded.

'Had it for years. Teddy checked it out last night around ten. It was clean. The filth busted into it sometime later and found it full of drugs. Like I said, half a million quid's worth. Now you know that's ridiculous, Nick. Anyone who knows me knows that. A little draw in the old days, but beak, no. It's not my game. The law beat down the door of my house at six this morning. They took Teddy down the station but had nothing on him and let him go. He came straight to me.'

'Are you sure?' I asked.

'What?'

'That he checked the place.'

'Sure I'm sure.'

'Could he have something to do with the drugs? A little private enterprise maybe?'

'Behave, Nick. He's family.'

'So was Hamlet, and look what happened to his mum and dad.'

Emerald looked disgusted. 'Nice try, Nick, but it doesn't add up. Teddy knew where I was last night, and if he wanted to cross me he could have sent Old Bill round anytime. And for that matter he knows where I am now. If he wanted me out of it, he could have sent them instead of bringing you.'

I shrugged. 'Just a thought, Em. They can't all be winners. I was thinking aloud. So who's in the frame?'

He shrugged back at me.

'Don't fuck about, Em. Someone is stitching you up good and proper, to the tune of half a mill. Even at the sort of street value the Old Bill throw around to make themselves look good, that's a lot of blow to throw away just to put your black backside in a sling.'

He grinned for the first time. 'You put it well, Nick, and you're right.'

'So?'

'There's a lot of people would like to see me banged up and the key thrown away.'

'I'm sure. Anyone in particular?'

'Bim,' said Emerald.

'Oh shit, no, not him,' I said, and thought about the name that Emerald had dropped into my lap like a bad moussaka. Bim. Bim the Greek. Bimpson Lupino. AKA 'The Uncrowned King Of South London Fruit and Veg'. Don't laugh. He earned the name the hard way.

Bim and his little firm, which he runs from his HQ, an acre or so of warehouse space at Nine Elms Market, have a monopoly on soft fruit, salad produce and every other sort of veggie you can name from Putney to the Blackwall Tunnel, and south to Croydon and beyond. Along with the wholesale vegetables, he owns half a dozen pubs and a couple of restaurants.

It's the old rags to riches story. Bim arrived from Greece straight after the war, owning just the clothes he stood up in. Only he didn't get a paper round or collect pop bottles for the deposits. Instead he met a recently demobbed soldier at Waterloo Station with a US Army issue Colt .45 to sell. As soon as the squaddie turned his back, Bim hit him on the head with a brick, stole the gun and used it to rob fourteen post offices in eight days. Bim did his first and last hard time then. Six years with a third off for good behaviour.

He was out of Wandsworth just as the fifties dragged themselves into view. By the time the sixties arrived, so had Bim. On the way, some people died. That's life. They would have to have died sooner or later, I suppose. Since then Bim's married twice and fathered six children, all girls. He has made a fortune or two in his time, and woe betide anyone who gets in his way. Now it seemed he was feuding with Emerald and that didn't bode well for anyone who interfered. And Em was asking *me* to get involved. I mean I'd heard about people who interfered with Bim's plans. There was an old joke about the meat pies served in the boozers he owned. They were made on the premises and I had an acquaintance who swore blind he'd found a human ear in one once, complete with a diamond stud that had paid for a new carburettor for his Cortina. All I know is, I stick to name brands for my steak and kidney these days. Talk about the devil and the deep blue sea.

'So what's he after?' I asked.

'My business. My places are good places, the best, that's why he wants them. A lot of cash comes through the doors every day. He's been after me to sell for a year. I want you to roust that bastard.'

'Just like that. You never mentioned Bim. He's fucking serious, man. Roust him – I should be so lucky! He kills people and I'm not at all well. I don't know about all this.'

'Are you scared?'

'Course I am.'

'You disappoint me.'

'It's the story of my life.'

'If you're not going to help, get the fuck out.'

'Come on, Em, don't be like that.'

'How else should I be?'

I fidgeted in my seat. I wasn't ready for any aggro. I *was* scared. I'd been hurt once too often to want to be hurt again. I'd promised myself a quiet life with lots of sex, and what was I getting?

'What about you, Em?' I asked. 'What are you going to do?'

'I'm going to give myself up.'

'You're crazy.'

'I've got no place else to go. I'm a respectable citizen, a businessman of some standing in the community. Besides, I thought you'd be looking out for me. I'm innocent, Nick, and I was counting on you to prove it.'

'I was serious about the brief.'

'Yeah, I know. I spoke to mine this morning.'

'And?'

'He thinks I should turn myself in too. It looks good. I just don't want to do it local. As well as friends, I've got a lot of enemies on the force.'

'All right,' I said reluctantly. 'For what it's worth, I'm your man. I just hope I don't live to regret it. Or die to regret it, for that matter.'

'So do I.'

'And you're determined to give yourself up?'

Emerald nodded.

'How about Danny Fox?' I said. 'Remember him?'

'How could I forget?'

'He's back in uniform down in Surrey, Farnham. He's a Superintendent now. Give yourself up to him. He won't pass you back to the Met without a fight. No one gets a prisoner off Danny Fox if he doesn't want to give him up.'

'It's an idea.'

'If you're determined to go through with it, it's the only idea. I don't want to see you getting beaten up in some holding cell, and then getting assaulting a police officer put on your sheet along with everything else. You're too old and ugly to take it these days.'

'Not so much of the old. I'll talk to Lupus and Teddy. Put them in the picture. You talk to Teddy too, Nick. He's not a bad boy, just trying to prove himself a man. He'll fill you in on any details. I'll get him to drive you home.'

'Good,' I said. 'It's not getting any drier out there.' I looked through the window again and could see the rain pouring down beyond the shelter of the motorway parapet. It beat down as if it wanted to wash West London off the map. Perhaps the rain had the right idea.

I heard a klaxon in the distance. Emerald tilted his head until it faded away. I don't know why he bothered. We both knew that if the police came for him, there would be no sirens advertising the fact. He tapped on the dividing glass again. It rolled down and the driver stuck his face through the gap.

'Boss?'

'Get Lupus and Teddy,' Emerald ordered.

The driver left the partition down and scrambled out of the car. He opened the back door of the Lincoln, held a short conversation and trotted back. The guy in the light mac and Lupus left the car and followed him over to where Emerald and I were waiting. I lit another cigarette.

Lupus yanked the back door of the Mercedes open and climbed in between Emerald and me. Teddy stayed outside. I blew smoke into his face.

'What's up?' he asked.

'Up?' asked Emerald back. 'What's up is that Mr Sharman is an old friend who is going to help us and you dissed him when you should have shown respect, that's what's up.'

Teddy looked away and sucked his teeth like he couldn't give a shit.

'Teddy,' said Em, 'you may be a big boy but if I get out of this car I'm going to slap you 'til you cry. Now apologise to Mr Sharman.'

Teddy's face suffused with blood.

'Leave it, Em,' I said.

To me: 'No.' To Teddy: 'Apologise, boy, when I tell you.'

Teddy pulled his mouth tight until his lips were as thin as razor blades. He looked at me as if I smelt bad. 'I'm sorry,' he spat.

'Forget it,' I said.

'Right,' said Emerald. 'Now remember, Teddy, Mr Sharman is a friend.'

'How's he going to help?' asked Lupus, giving me a dirty look. It didn't worry me, I was getting used to it.

'He's going to find out who planted the dope.'

'We can do that,' protested Lupus. 'Don't you trust us?'

'Of course I do,' said Emerald. 'I need you to take care of business. We need cash flow. Keep everything going, that's your job. Nick used to be law. He can do these things better.' He turned towards the younger man. 'Teddy, take Mr Sharman home, use the Bee-Em. And tell him anything he wants to know.'

Teddy gave me another disgusted look. 'What about JonJo? He's the driver.'

'Teddy, who I say is the driver, is the driver. Right?'

'Right, Uncle.' I thought Teddy might salute.

'And Teddy?'

'Yes.'

'Be friendly.'

Teddy nodded, but still looked daggers at me. I was getting bored with his attitude.

'I'll sit in the front with you,' I said. 'It'll be cosy, just the two of us.'

Teddy turned his back on me and stalked towards the smallest of the three cars. I shook Emerald's hand. 'Take care,' I said.

'I will.'

I nodded at Lupus. 'I'll be in touch.'

He grunted.

I took my stick and joined Teddy in the BMW.

6

I opened the door and hiked myself in, pushing my
stick into the well under the dash. Teddy switched
on the engine and it caught with a whisper. He put
the car into gear and we crunched across the loose
surface towards the gate into the street. He
stopped the car and looked at me. I looked back.

'You want to open the gates?' he asked.

I shook my head and touched my stick with my
foot. 'Excused heavy duties.'

'Maybe so, but I need to know that the street is
clear. If there's a copper outside I don't want to
be stuck half in and half out with Uncle back
there.'

I saw the logic. 'OK,' I said, and left my stick
and climbed out of the car again. I pulled one of
the gates maybe a foot wide and checked the
street. The rain was pouring down and bouncing
off the tarmac like bullets. The street was empty
for as far as I could see and I pulled the gate wide.
It was damned awkward with my bad leg and all.
I had to lean on the wood for balance as I did it
and I was getting soaked. I waved Teddy through
and he pulled the BMW into the roadway. I
dragged the gate shut behind me and limped over
to the car feeling the rain beating on my skull. I

got back in and dragged my fingers through my hair, squeezing some of the water out as I went. Teddy snapped the car away from the kerb and plunged it through the puddles heading south.

I nicked a peek in his direction as we joined the main road. Teddy's skin was almost luminous with health. It was stretched over high cheek-bones and his nose was more European than African in appearance. His hair was cropped to a flat top and the sides shaven close enough to the skin on his skull for the veins to show. All in all he was a pretty good-looking guy, except for his ugly expression.

'Don't pout, Teddy,' I said. 'The wind might change and your face will stay that way.'

He made a disgusted sound and turned the radio on. The inside of the car was filled with the sound of a girl not much older than my own daughter singing about underage sex. I wondered what we were coming to and stabbed the mute button. Teddy looked like he wanted to hit me. 'Relax,' I said. 'You're stuck with me now. Uncle Em has invited me to join the firm for a bit, so why don't you make the best of it?'

'What can you do that we can't?'

I wasn't sure. 'Don't ask me, ask Emerald,' was all I said.

Teddy was silent.

'I need a drink and something to eat. Join me?'

'You're the boss,' he sneered.

'Yeah,' I said to make sure he remembered it.

We crossed the river and hit the South Circular and I directed him to a small restaurant-cum-bar I use in West Norwood. It fed my Rolling Rock habit, was usually quiet around lunchtime and did a decent all-day breakfast when the chef wasn't having a nervous breakdown.

Teddy parked on a single yellow line and walked in front of me through the rain to the door. He yanked the collar of his coat up around his ears as if it would cut me out of his life. It didn't. When he looked round I was still there.

We pushed into the warm interior of the place and Teddy shrugged out of his raincoat and hung it on the rack. I did the same with my overcoat. Underneath his coat he was wearing a baggy, double-breasted suit over a pale shirt and a wildly patterned tie. He slumped down in one of the stools in front of the long, fancy-tiled bar and I joined him. As I'd thought, the place was nearly empty. The weather was keeping the folks at home. There were two people eating in the restaurant section, another couple drinking at one of the bar tables, and one young guy whom I was on nodding acquaintance with sitting at the far end of the bar, staring into a glass of beer. He looked up when we entered and half raised his hand in greeting to me, but left us alone.

The fox behind the bar sashayed to the fridge, bent down and pulled out a bottle of Rock, showing us the tops of her breasts. She held up the bottle for my approval. When I nodded she snapped off the top and put the bottle and a glass down on the bar in front of me.

I smiled. 'Thanks,' I said. 'What about you, Teddy?'

'The same.'

The barmaid turned and hauled another bottle

out, all without saying a word. 'How's things?' I inquired of her.

'Can't complain. You?'

'I've had a lovely morning. I've been to Notting Hill.'

'Lucky old you. I've always thought it was one of the few places that made Norwood look good.'

'I couldn't agree more,' I said, and paid for the drinks.

The owner of the bar stuck his head out of the kitchen door, saw me and walked over. 'How are you today?'

'Fine,' I replied. 'I brought a friend with me. This is Teddy.'

'Hi, I'm Simon,' said the owner. 'You're very welcome. Are you eating?'

I nodded and he reeled off the day's specials, but I opted for egg, bacon, sausage and mushrooms, with toast and coffee on the side. Teddy took the same and Simon went back to the kitchen. The barmaid retreated to her perch beside the coffee machine and stuck her head in a Jackie Collins paperback.

I turned to Teddy. 'Listen,' I said, 'if we're going to help Em, we're going to have to lose this attitude problem. I don't care how we do it, but unless it goes we're wasting time. You want to take a walk outside and bang heads or do you want to have a friendly drink and be nice?'

At first it looked as if he might go for the fight option and my heart sank, but after a moment he picked up his bottle of beer, half filled his glass and raised it in a salute. 'If I'm stuck with you, I'm stuck with you, I guess. Uncle thinks it's cool, so be it. Cheers.'

I grinned. 'Cheers, Teddy,' I said and returned the salute.

He sipped at his drink. 'I apologise for riding you. I was out of order,' he said. 'It's been a rough morning.'

'Apology accepted.' I held out my hand. After a moment he took it and we shook hands.

'Oh, hell,' he said. 'You'll do.'

I grinned. 'You too.' He grinned back and it was OK between us.

Simon brought the food and we ate at the bar. We were both starving and the food tasted better than good. We emptied our plates without talking. I finished my coffee and lit a cigarette and ordered two more beers. Teddy was a beat behind me and pushed his plate away with a satisfied smile. 'Great,' he said. 'I feel better for that. I hardly slept and I haven't eaten since last night. Old Bill hauled me down the station when it was still pitch dark.'

'I'm glad to see you had time to slip into something elegant,' I said, glancing at his suit.

'This is last night's, it's all creased to shit.'

'Never mind, you look a picture.'

He grinned again. 'Scene,' he said.

I changed the subject. 'Let's get down to facts,' I said.

'Firstly, what brought about your uncle's change of fortune?'

'He got lucky.'

'Some people might think he got into heavy duty drug dealing. He's got all the trappings.'

'No, he got lucky.'

'Tell me about it.'

'How long since you've seen him?'

'Eighteen months or so.' I remembered exactly. It was hard to forget, but I didn't tell Teddy that. 'He just had the club then. The place in Clapham, and the girls of course, and he was being minded by a bunch of Rastas.'

'That wasn't all he had,' said Teddy.

'Like?'

'Well, you know he came over here in '48?' I could see that I was in for a history lesson, which I didn't really need, but the first rule of interrogation that I had learned was: when someone wants to tell a story, let them.

'Yeah,' I said.

'He was on one of the first immigrant ships. He was just a kid – twelve, I think. They dumped him and his mum and dad, and my dad, that's his little brother, he was just a tiny baby then, in the station at Brixton. Fucking government! The middle of winter and they put them on camp beds in a freezing railway station, and them just in from JA. You know all that?'

'Some,' I said.

'Well, Uncle Watkins got mad. He wasn't going to grow up and put on no bus conductor's uniform. He catered for the immigrants. He started off running errands, never went to school, learnt his shit on the street. My grandpa and grandma went spare but he paid no attention. As soon as he was old enough, he started a shebeen. Fucking fifteen-year-old kid selling beer and home-made rum to grown men. A few tried to take it off him, but he had mates. Black youth has always been tough. They fought the cops and the old men and Teddy Boys and all sorts. Won too.'

Teddy looked proud of his uncle and I didn't blame him. Times had been tough then, were now, and always would be, Amen.

'When he got some dough,' Teddy went on, 'he started buying houses. Put the Brothers in. Fair rents, believe it or not. In those days blacks were being refused accommodation just for being black. "No coloureds" signs in the windows, just like South Africa. So Uncle Watkins helped out. He bought houses all over Brixton. He was a funny cat. Figured that if the white government dumped him and his in Brixton, they must want him to own the place, and I believe he nearly did. Brothers owe him.'

I interrupted. 'I heard some of this, Teddy. Don't make him out to be Albert Schweitzer. He was a slum landlord, running whores and bad liquor on the side.'

'Shit, I never said he was no saint,' protested Teddy. 'But it was better that Uncle Watkins ran the housing than fucking Jew landlords or Malts or Greeks or Irish, or fucking Pinkies for that matter. You know how those bastards, you bastards –' he grinned to soften the words, but I knew he still meant them '– treated the Brothers and Sisters. Worse than shit. At least Uncle Watkins kept the toilets flushing and the roofs in one piece.'

'So?' I asked.

'Oh, yeah. Anyway, he bought and sold hundreds of houses over the years.' He paused to light a cigarette. 'You sure you don't know all this?'

'Like I said, some. But you tell me anyway.'

'So he bought and sold and ran the girls and the

drinkers and the shpeilers and eventually he sold everything but the club and one street of houses and shops, and then a year or so ago he sold the street in one lot and they built a supermarket there.'

'Where?'

'Down by the town hall. And he made some dough out of it, let me tell you.'

'You don't mean . . . ?' I asked.

He nodded.

'I don't believe it.'

'God's truth.'

'So that little street bought him a new Lincoln?'

'And a house, three pubs and a Caribbean restaurant.'

'Straight businesses?'

'As a die.'

'Jesus! I hope they kept the foundations light. You never know what you'll find buried under one of Emerald's houses.' Or who, I thought, but didn't bother to add that.

Teddy laughed and ordered more beer. As the barmaid served us I turned and looked through the big windows of the bar at the empty, rainswept streets and shivered despite the warmth inside.

'So where does Bim come in?' I asked when fresh beers arrived in front of us.

'They've been enemies for years. Now Uncle Watkins got legit pubs and a restaurant it's open warfare. You know how it started?'

I shook my head.

'Sprouts, man.'

'Sprouts?'

'Fucking Brussel sprouts. Bim used to supply uncle with fruit and veg years ago, when he had his old place. One Christmas there's a delivery of Brussel sprouts. I mean a truckload. Stupid guy in the kitchen takes them in and signs for them. Uncle hits the roof. He's ordered a bag of sprouts, like, you know, fifty pounds. Gets a gross of bags. Tries to send them back. Bim won't take them. I swear those sprouts went across London from New Year to Easter. And man they're starting to go rotten, like they're almost liquid and they stink. But those two guys are so stubborn neither will give in. Eventually Uncle has them dumped on Bim's front lawn. His wife near had a fit. They almost started a shooting war over a couple of grand's worth of vegetables. That's how crazy they are. Bim don't like black men, especially on his turf.' He blew air. 'Man, it's anybody's turf out there, right?'

'Right. So tell me all about this lock up in Wandsworth.'

Teddy shook his head sadly. 'Uncle doesn't own it, just rents it. At one time he was thinking about running a cab firm from down there. He would have had a workshop and offices, but nothing came of it. The rent is dirt cheap, it's on a long lease from the railway, and he just never bothered to let it go. He stores old shit down there. It's just a dump really.'

'And?'

'And when Lupus and I were checking last night, everything was cool. I drove down there.'

'On your own?' I interrupted.

'Yeah, we split the premises for speed. We

needed to work fast. It was the last place I went to. I didn't even realise anyone else outside the firm knew about it. It only gets used once in a blue moon.'

'Someone knew.'

'Someone did, and to let me go in and come out again before they planted the gear.'

'What exactly happened?'

'How do you mean?'

'Just that. What did you do? Run me through it.'

He thought for a second. 'I went down around ten. I had my own car. There's a slip road off the Wandsworth Road. Our place is the last arch, right where the road ends. Then there's a bit of pavement, some grass, a fence and the back of a council estate. It's dark down there, the street lights are crap. I parked the car facing the door, headlights on full. There's a set of big double doors that open right up so's you can drive a truck in, and there's a small door set into one of them. The little door is locked by a Yale and a padlock. They were both tight. I had the keys and I opened up, put the lights on and took a look round. Like I said, it's a dump. Boxes and crap everywhere. It didn't look as if anyone had been there for months. I checked the downstairs office and the little one upstairs too. There was nothing there I could see. I swear there was nothing there. I mean, man, I didn't even know what I was looking for, but there was definitely no drug paraphernalia. It was quiet and bloody freezing. I locked up again and left, and went straight to Uncle's to stay like he asked me to. I sat up 'til three watching TV and got my head down on the sofa. At six Old Bill came in with sledgehammers. You know the rest.'

'Someone knew you'd check.'

'Looks like it.'

'Who exactly?'

'Whoever tipped Uncle. It was an anonymous call. Could have been anyone. They said they were mens, but who knows?'

'Your uncle was sure they were.'

'Buzz words. Anyone can use them.

'Like who?'

'Like anyone who wants to see Uncle stiffed. Like the Rastas he dumped when he sold out to the developers. Lupus reckoned they lowered the tone of the organisation. They could have cooked the whole thing up with Bim and told him about the lock-up out of spite.'

'They wouldn't have been too pleased about being rowed out of the action just when it got sweet, I grant you,' I said.

'Uncle was a bit iffy about it, too. He's loyal, but Lupus kept on at him and eventually Uncle gave in so Lupus done the deed.'

'Yeah, Lupus. I've been wondering about him. Where the hell did he spring from?'

'Don't know. He was there before Uncle Watkins took me on. Clever man. Lawyer and accountant.'

'I thought I didn't like him. What's he do for Em?'

'A bit of everything. He's like the number two man.'

'And you don't mind? Being family and all.'

Teddy looked at me through slitted eyes. 'I don't give a shit,' he said. 'I know what's coming to me.

So long as I got cash and some good gear on my back and nice wheels to drive, I'm OK.'

I didn't believe a word of that. 'So you just kick back and catch the scraps from the table?'

'Don't be stupid,' said Teddy dismissively. 'I do well. Uncle Watkins looks after his family.'

'I'm pleased to hear it,' I said. 'What were you doing before Em took you on?'

'Me, man? I was ducking and diving. Doing odd jobs, looking for deals.'

'Save it, Teddy,' I said. 'You talk street, but a lot of your vocabulary comes from somewhere else. So don't jive me, Bro.'

'Shit, boss,' he said, 'you got me. I passed my "A" levels and read sociology at Bristol. Uncle took care of me. He's been good and now I can help him, pay a bit back.'

'You can help me if you want.'

'I'll do what I can. What do you think will happen to Uncle?'

'It could go very bad for him.'

'He's done nothing.'

'It was a lot of dope to leave lying about.'

'Sure was.'

'Too much just to frame Em, that's the trouble. It's severe overkill. A couple of grand's worth could have done that. It'll look bad in court.'

'He's got an excellent lawyer.'

'I'm sure, but I bet he doesn't get bail.'

'So what can you do?'

'Make inquiries. That's my job. I'll start this afternoon. Will you drop me home?'

'Sure.'

'You'd better pay the bill then and we can go.'

'Am I paying for yours?'

'Sure. I'm doing Em a favour, but it doesn't include feeding his family.'

'Generous man.'

'You'd better believe it.'

He called over the barmaid and paid our bill and we pulled on our coats again and went back through the rain to the car. I directed Teddy to my place and he dropped me outside. I left him one of my cards and told him to call me later.

7

I went upstairs to my flat and cracked a beer, lit a
cigarette and sat down by the phone. I called West
End Central and spoke to the one copper who had
come to see me in hospital when he didn't have to.

His name was Endesleigh, Detective Inspector
Endesleigh. An amazingly senior rank for someone
so young. He always looked as if he should have
been at school studying for his GCSEs, but he was a
good copper and for some reason we were friends.
On my side, perhaps because he had once saved
my life. On his side, I didn't have a clue. I caught
him at his desk.

'Endesleigh,' he said.

'Good afternoon.'

'Sharman, how's life?'

'All right, but I could do with your help.'

'I don't like the sound of that. Why, you got a
parking ticket you want me to fix?'

'I'm working.'

'Are you serious?'

'Of course.'

'What the hell are you doing?'

'I'm helping an old friend.'

'Who?'

'Samuel Watkins.'

'I'm none the wiser.'

'He's also known as Emerald.'

'Yeah, wait a minute, that rings a bell.'

'He's being done for intent to supply Class-A drugs, cocaine, a half a million pounds' worth. Warrants were issued last night sometime.'

'I think I heard about it. He's some old super-annuated South London face isn't he?'

'I don't think he'd be too fond of the description, but yes I suppose you could say that.'

'He's on the run, isn't he?'

'Yes.'

'And you're helping him.'

'Yes.'

'So you've seen him?'

'That's right.'

'Sharman, you do put yourself on offer, don't you?'

'He's going to give himself up. Might even have done it by now.'

'Good plan.'

'To Danny Fox.'

'This gets better and better. Why him?'

'Emerald's not in love with the idea of the Met taking care of his accommodation needs for the foreseeable future.'

'Was that your idea?'

'Yes.'

'You won't win any popularity contests.'

'I'll survive.'

'Don't be so sure.'

'That's not the point.'

'What is?'

'He's innocent.'

Endesleigh choked back a laugh. 'Tell me about it! Someone else left half a million's worth of coke on your friend's premises? Careless, wouldn't you say? Especially on the very night the drug squad had nothing better to do.'

'That place was clean at ten last night. Christ, Endesleigh. Emerald had been tipped off. He had an anonymous call purporting to be from one of your own. He'd be pretty stupid not to send in a clean-up team. He had plenty of time.'

'You've got my attention.'

'Besides, he's not into coke,' I insisted.

'Sez who?'

'Him. And me, for that matter. He never has been in all the years I've known him.'

'Tell that to the jury.'

'Come on,' I said. 'Never heard of a stitch up?'

'And if he's a friend of yours it would be?'

'In this case, yes.'

'And who's the stitcher?'

'Bimpson Lupino, he thinks.'

Endesleigh stifled another laugh. 'This gets better. All those old bastards are due the retirement home. It'll be Ronnie and Reggie next. Give me a break! Give yourself a break. Claim industrial injuries and get lost. Take a holiday.'

'I am giving you a break,' I said. 'You could do yourself a bit of good.'

'How?'

'If it *was* a copper who told Emerald, then one of your boys is bent, if it wasn't . . .'

'If it wasn't I'm not interested.'

'But it had to come from inside the squad whoever tipped him off.'

'If anyone did. Perhaps he's just blowing smoke in your face. Perhaps he's telling porkies.'

'Why should he?'

'How the hell do I know? He's in a bind. Wouldn't you?'

'But why me? I'm not the DPP.'

'That's for you to find out. Now listen, I like you, Sharman, I really do. But, sorry, not interested.'

'And if I can get you some proof?'

'That, of course, is a different matter. But it'll have to be good, I'll be treading on serious toes.'

'I'll come back to you.'

'Be careful.'

'Your concern is touching.'

'I like you alive. You're the original "There but for the grace of God" man.'

'Sweet,' I said. 'Look, I've got to go. I'll be talking to you.'

'I wait with bated breath.'

8

I put down the phone, and picked it straight up again and called Fiona. We had a date for that evening and I wanted to tell her what had gone down. She was working on a session for the *Star*. I got through to the photographer's studio and climbed rung by rung from the receptionist to the photographer's assistant.

I asked if Fiona was free and the sniffy boy who answered blew something nasal down the phone, dropped it on to a hard surface and abandoned me. I waited for two or three minutes, listening to a *Pet Shop Boys* tape interspersed with laughter and screaming, before the receiver was picked up again. I heard the sound of Fiona's voice. 'Hello,' she shouted above the din.

'Hello,' I said.

'Sharman, how are you?'

'I'm fine.'

'What sort of day have you had?'

'Usual physiotherapy, then I was kidnapped and driven halfway across London in a limo full of crazy spades, met an old friend who's looking at a double handful of porridge for drug dealing, had egg and bacon for lunch and I think it's giving me indigestion. Apart from that, nothing special. How was yours?'

'Terrific,' said Fiona dryly. 'I met a little green man from Alpha Centauri on the way to work and he asked me to elope in his flying saucer.'

Typical, I thought. Some days you tell the truth and no one will believe a word. 'Very funny,' was all I said, and she just carried on as if she mixed every day with people who got kidnapped.

'No, but I did meet this geezer I used to know. He lives in the flats at the back of my dad's. His name's Johnny, Johnny Smoke.'

I never knew if she was taking the rise. 'What does he do?' I interrupted. 'Work in a merchant bank?'

'No, don't piss about, I'm serious. He's a DJ, does some pubs and clubs. He's having a Christmas do in a boozer I used to go to, The Pig in Tower Bridge. I said we'd pop in later for a drink. Is that all right?'

A Thursday night in a pub in Tower Bridge, ten days before Christmas, I ask you. 'Fine by me,' I said. Well, you have to, don't you?

'Yeah, I thought it was about time you got out and about again. You're growing roots in front of the TV. I'll call round for you about eight, and we'll get straight up there. It'll get a bit crowded later on. They've got a two o'clock licence, see.'

A two o'clock licence in the East End. Jesus, my cup runneth over. 'Sure,' I said. 'Why don't you come round about six and we'll think about it?'

'No chance. I don't think this wally's ever going to get my tits right. He's been poncing about with them since twelve.'

'I wish I could ponce around with your tits for a few hours,' I said almost wistfully.

'Later. We'll hang around for an hour or so at the boozer, then get something to eat up West and back to mine, and you can do whatever you like with my tits.'

'I can't wait.'

'Tell me about it. Listen, I'm being shouted at, I'd better go. I'll see you at eight, all right?'

'All right,' I said back, but she was gone. Lovely girl but a bit of an organiser. Mind you, I didn't care. With a figure like hers she could organise the hell out of me.

The rest of the afternoon I spent on the phone. I went through my book from A–Z. I spoke to anyone I could think of who might have any relevant information. Although Em being on the run was the talk of the manor, no one seemed to know what was going on, or if they did they weren't talking. At least not to me, and not on the phone. I knew I was going to have to put on my travelling shoes and visit a few boozers and put the fear of God into a few faces. But I didn't want to be out when Teddy rang with the full SP on his uncle.

Teddy called me at seven. He told me that Em had surrendered to Danny Fox at Farnham with his brief in tow. I told him I was on the case and to call me next morning, hung up and took a shower.

At eight the doorbell rang. I had dressed to get down. Blue silk suit with just a hint of shine in the material, pale blue shirt, a tie patterned with red roses and black, soft loafers which fitted over my sore foot without too much angst. I checked the weather, put on my trench coat with the button-in winter lining and limped down the stairs.

Fiona was standing on the doorstep. She was all

bundled up in a long navy overcoat that reached nearly to her ankles. She had a long muffler wrapped six or seven times around her neck and her hair was pushed up under a big black hat. She was wearing black, high-heeled shoes. I hated it when she drove in heels, but she looked so sexy I almost wept.

'Cold, is it?' I asked.

'Not many. At least it's stopped raining.'

'Why don't you get a top for that car?'

'No, I'll survive, I'm hard.'

I raised my eyes to heaven, but she didn't notice and I followed her over to the little yellow bug that sat at the kerbside. We clambered in and the engine started with a cough and a whine. She took off like a rocket, without looking or indicating, and cut up a geezer in a Capri who gave us a long blast on his horn. Fiona waved in a friendly way and I shrank down in my bucket seat.

'What's all this about being kidnapped?' she asked over the rattle of the engine and the roar of the wind.

I told her the whole story which took as far as the Elephant, and she digested the information whilst she chopped through the late evening traffic up to the river. She parked the car in a side street and we went arm in arm up to the main road.

'And you agreed to help?' she asked as we walked, or rather as she walked and I hobbled.

'Sure.'

'Why?'

'That's what friends are for.'

'I hope you know what you're doing. Christ, Bim and Em,' she said. 'Sounds like a double act, or something out of the *Beano*.' She cackled at the thought.

'Don't be fooled,' I said. 'Those two are serious, dead serious.'

She shrugged and we passed under the street lamps to the corner. The Pig was a big old Victorian gin palace, set back on a sort of double pavement on a tree-lined boulevard that ran up to the river. Most of the old houses in the street had gone and been replaced by glass matchboxes laid on their sides. The Victorian pub stood out like a sore finger. It wasn't exactly beautiful or particularly welcoming but it certainly had it over the sawn-off skyscrapers that dominated the rest of the street. From the outside the pub looked like any other local in the area, but by the look of the cars parked nearby it certainly wasn't an ordinary local where the poor came to eke out their twilight years. There was a big green Rolls-Royce, three or four XR3is, Golfs, Jeeps, and a couple of battered old Yanks parked on and by the pavement.

Fiona pushed the door of the pub open and we got a blast of *Blue Monday* and a faceful of warm air that smelt in equal parts of tobacco, perfume and beer. Well, maybe the perfume won by a short head. She held the door open and I hopped in. Some habits never change, whatever the clientele. As the door opened, like a crowd at the centre court, every head in the bar turned towards it. It happened every time, all evening. Sometimes an entrance would merit a yell of recognition, other times the cold shoulder. We got half and half. Guess who got recognised and who got ignored? My limp got more attention than I did. There was a free table in one corner and we grabbed the seats.

'What do you want?' I asked.

'I'll get them in, there's a couple of people up at the bar I know.' She pulled off her hat and scarf and coat and dumped them on her seat. Underneath she was wearing a black leather suit over what looked suspiciously like a lavender lace corset. On her legs she wore lavender nylons.

She noticed me clocking the outfit. 'Do you like my teddy?' she asked.

'My daughter takes one to bed with her.'

'Well, maybe you'll get lucky and take one to bed with you tonight.'

'Just don't take your jacket off, you'll start a riot,' I said.

She grinned wickedly and leant over and planted a kiss on my cheek. 'I know,' she said. 'And you've got lipstick all over your face.'

I gave her a big, false grin and swatted at my face with the back of my hand. 'I'll have a pint, and don't be all night.'

'You're so masterful,' she said, and vanished into the crowd.

I shrugged out of my raincoat and hung it over the back of a red velour-covered chair, then sat down and wedged my bad foot on to the rung of a small stool opposite me. My leg was killing me and I massaged it with my hand. I looked round the bar. It was a young crowd, with just a few old codgers sprinkled about, looking lost and forlorn as their old boozer got taken over by the Snakebite and Pina Colada set.

It was a big old Victorian gin palace on the outside and it was a big old Victorian gin palace on the inside. The ceilings were high and tobacco-stained, with red-shaded lamps hanging down. The walls were covered with flock wallpaper and dotted with sporting prints. There were tables with seating for fifty or sixty. The bar itself was U-shaped, long, solid and polished. Every surface in the place was hung with Christmas decorations. There must have been a grand's worth of tinsel. A twenty-foot Christmas tree, dripping with lights, stood next to the juke-box. From half a dozen vantage points Sandra and Frank wished me the compliments of the season from under a photograph of a bullet-headed heavy and a tiny blonde dripping with gold. The real pair were dispensing drinks and cockney bonhomie from the opposite side of the bar.

Right beside me was a raised podium, like a small stage. A bloke in blue jeans and a psychedelic shirt was setting up a twin turntable plugged through a bank of amplifiers, linked to some dangerous-looking speakers which made it obvious why the table we'd nicked had been vacant.

Shit, I thought.

Fiona had a hard time getting to the bar, she was so popular. She must have stopped and chewed the fat with about a dozen faces on the way to the counter. Most of the characters who buttonholed her gave me the once over. I nodded back a couple of times but soon gave it a rest. My leg still hurt and I wanted a drink.

She was grabbed round the waist by a bloke sitting on a stool at the end of the bar, close to the public telephone. Their heads were about level and he whispered something into her ear and pulled a Harrods bag up from the floor and gave her a squint inside. She laughed and shook her head and gave him a cuddle. He was dark-skinned and balding. I didn't know him, but I knew he was bent, not that I cared. If I'd ever been inside a villain's pub, this was it.

Finally she shucked off the old pals and connected with the barman. In less time than it takes to tell she came over to the table with a couple of glasses.

'Sorry,' she said.

I shrugged. 'Old home week?'

'Sort of. I know a lot of people here.'

'You don't say.'

'Here's your drink.'

'Thanks.'

She pushed her hat and coat over and sat down opposite me.

'Who was the affectionate one?' I asked.

'Who?'

I pointed at him with a glance.

'Oh, him. He's harmless. Mickey Lipman. He fences for the hoisters. I thought you might know him.'

'Do you think I know every lowlife in London?'

'No, you just look like you do.' And she stuck out her tongue.

She looked around and then up at the geezer who was setting up the audio equipment on the stage. 'Phil!' she said by way of a greeting.

He looked twice, then connected. 'Fi,' he said back, and hunkered down on to his boot heels. 'How are you doing?'

'All right,' she replied, and sank a third of the

contents of her glass in one gulp. 'Meet Nick.' She gestured to me.

'Hello,' I said.

'Hello,' he said back, extending his hand. I shook it.

'Phil's Johnny's roadie,' said Fiona by way of explanation. 'Where is he?' she asked.

'He'll be along,' said Phil. 'With his box of records, just in time for the show. You know he likes to make a big entrance.'

I got the feeling Phil thought that Johnny Smoke had an overinflated reputation, especially with young women, especially the type who wore lavender lace teddies.

'Don't be bitchy, Phil,' said Fiona. 'He is the star of the show.'

'Sure,' said Phil. 'I'd better get on with setting up the gear.' He climbed to his feet and and went back to tinkering with leads and amps.

'Happy little soul,' I said.

'He wants to be a star,' said Fiona.

'Don't we all?'

As if on cue the door to the pub burst open and an apparition in a yellow, hooded T-shirt with an Italian flag printed across the front, purple-flowered tight Bermudas, white-framed Ray-Bans and orange baseball boots leapt through the gap and into the light.

'Heeeeere's Johnny,' said Fiona.

'I never would have guessed.'

Johnny was a star all right, and he loved it. He ran from one group of his fans to another, shaking hands, touching shoulders, generally being a right pain in the arse. Eventually he turkey trotted over to our table. 'Fiona, sweety poopy! So glad you could make it.' He pushed the Ray Bans over the top of his gelled hair. 'And you must be Nicky Baby. Heard a lot about you kid, all good.'

I thought if he called me Nicky Baby again I'd plant the toe of my Shelley's special loafers right up the crack of his fat backside, bad leg or no bad leg. Fiona made a placating face behind his back. I gave in. What the hell? If it made her happy I guessed I could take Johnny Smoke like bad medicine and smile all the time.

'Hi, Johnny,' I said. 'Nice to meet you.'

He pulled up a chair and sat down. He raised a finger and an acolyte attended with a bottle of Grolsch. Johnny went through a big production of flicking the top one-handed and everyone in the room admired his style. He drank from the bottle, how else? I half hoped the china top that was still attached to the bottle by a clever little metal contraption would put his eye out. After giving his full attention to the temperature of the beer for a second, he turned his charm on Fiona. 'How's the career, poopy baby?' he asked with all the sincerity of a life insurance salesman on Mogadon.

'Can't complain,' she said. 'How's yours?'

This was the question he had been waiting for. He flicked his head forward so the shades dropped back on to his nose and was away like the favourite at Harringay. 'C'est magnifique, baybee,' he said. 'Might be going to Marbella, get away from the weather.'

I felt like telling him he might be slightly warmer if he dressed for a British December rather than an Hawaiian June, but what the hell?

'Nice,' said Fiona.

'Yeah, I've been offered a residency at a big nightclub over there. One and a half K a week and all the puss I can handle.' Which from where I sat was precisely zip, but maybe I was jealous, just like Phil.

'Fuck off, Johnny,' said Fiona, bringing a welcome air of reality to the proceedings. 'You don't have to impress me, we're not at Stringfellow's now. I get that sort of bullshit all day at work. Lighten up and get some drinks in.'

Johnny pushed his Ray-Bans up over his forehead again and grinned. He held up his hands. 'I give in,' he said. 'You always could see through the old bollocks.' He turned to me. 'Don't let her go, Nick. She's as good as gold. Better than gold, in fact. What are you drinking?'

'I'll have a pint.'

'Cold Becks,' said Fiona.

Johnny was passing the order over to the bar when the front door swung open again. A swarthy-looking geezer in a long tweed overcoat over jeans tucked into polished riding boots crept through the doorway carrying a cardboard box under his arm. He had a mass of thick curly hair that he pushed back from his face as he sized up the crowd. He saw Johnny and made for him like he was on a piece of elastic.

'Fran-ches-co,' screamed Johnny, going straight back to being a jerk again.

'Hello, John,' the swarthy geezer said.

'My man,' said Johnny. 'Meet some friends. Francis, this is Fiona and Nick. Fiona and Nick this is Francis.'

There was no way you could fault the guy for
manners.

'Call me Frank,' said the swarthy geezer.

'Hello, Frank,' I said.

'Frank,' echoed Fiona.

Our drinks arrived over the bar. Frank looked
thirsty but no one offered to buy him a drink. He
kept looking at me and I toasted him with my glass.
It wasn't my round. He looked harder and when he
spoke I knew it wasn't a drink he was after, not
from me at any rate.

'You Babylon?' he demanded in pure Kingston,
JA.

Shit, I thought, another half lemonade giving me
fucking grief.

'Fuck off,' I said. 'Do I look like bleeding
Babylon?'

'Yes.'

'Private,' I said. 'And I'm on my holidays, so
relax. I ain't going to nick you.'

Frank still looked unhappy.

Johnny cut in, 'He's all right, Francis. A diamond.
He's with Fiona.'

Frank seemed happy with the explanation.
'Want to buy some gear then?' he asked.

'What you got?' asked Johnny.

'A new steam iron and six Filofaxes, great for
presents.'

'How much?' asked Johnny.

Frank pretended to do some mental sums,
although I knew he had the price fixed before he'd
lifted the stuff. 'Fifteen for the iron and a tenner
each for the Filofaxes. There's more than a
tenner's worth of filling in each one.'

Johnny shook his head sadly. 'No chance.'

'Oh, come on,' said Frank.

Johnny dug in the box. 'Take forty?' he asked.

Frank sighed deeply. 'Give us a break,' he said. 'Fifty, the lot.'

Johnny rotated his head like a turtle. 'All right, you got it.' He pulled out a roll of cash and peeled off five tens. Frank's hand ate the money like a snake swallowing a small mouse.

Mickey Lipman slid from his perch on the bar stool and on to the floor. He must have stood at least four feet nine. I swear he was taller sitting down. He pushed through the crowd. 'Hello, my loves,' he said. 'Hello, Frank.'

'Hello, Mickey,' said Frank. The rest of us didn't respond.

'Give,' said Mickey.

'What?' asked Frank.

'Don't fuck around. The dough.'

'Jesus, Mickey, do us a favour.' He looked around as if for divine intervention.

'Give.'

Frank reluctantly handed over the cash. Mickey counted it in less than a second. 'I'll take it off your bill,' he said.

'No, not all of it, I'm short. Give us some spends.'

'I'm short too,' said Mickey. He was right about that. There weren't many shorter in the room.

'Please,' begged Frank.

Mickey pulled a face. 'A tenner,' he said.

'Sweet.'

Mickey peeled off a single note and handed it back, then split.

Frank smiled. 'Want a drink?' he asked the

gathering. Johnny nodded, Fiona nodded, Frank looked at me.

'Not if you're skint,' I said. He looked at Mickey's retreating back and grinned.

' 'S'all right,' he said. 'I got a couple of watches in here.' He patted his coat pocket. 'I'll knock them out later. If Mickey don't see me, I'll be cool.'

I shrugged. 'You talked me into it.' I said. 'I'll have a beer.'

Frank went to the bar and Johnny Smoke took his box of bent gear out to his car.

'Nice boozer,' I said.

'It'll do. You see life.'

'You can say that again!'

'Don't go all copperish on me. You Babylon?' she mimicked Frank. 'I thought you were going to have kittens.'

Frank came back with the beers and Johnny came into the pub with two big boxes of records. He unloaded them on to Phil and boogied round the pub some more.

At ten o'clock the overhead lights in the pub dimmed which left only the bar, Christmas tree, juke box, pool table and a spot over the stage lit, and Johnny got to work. He was good, I'll give him that. Noisy, but good. I looked around the pub, through the gloom, and saw an amazing amount of traffic in and out of the Gents. It looked as if the boys were powdering their noses with a vengeance. And the girls? The girls were rolling joints on the tables and getting bombed on marijuana and Pernod until their brains cooked.

The big guy who ran the place could finally stand no more. He ran round the bar during a particularly frantic *Led Zep/Public Enemy* segue and confiscated a joint, then ran into the Gents to reappear with a crop-headed B-boy under each arm and summarily eject same from the pub.

Johnny bopped to the chaos. He soundtracked the swaying crew with tough black music from Chicago, jazz from the West Coast circa 1959, rare groove from Philly and Detroit, and pure pop from just about everywhere else. The place had filled to the extent that it was SRO, the punters were ten deep at the bar and the staff had run out of glasses. I blessed the foresight of being a couple of rounds in front.

The air in the room was as thick as soup and stank of dope and hairspray. The temperature was in the low nineties and still climbing. Moisture had condensed on the ceiling and was dripping down like acid rain that stained clothes and burnt skin. Johnny closed his first set with a *T-Rex* classic. The lights came up and the juke-box ground back into life in the middle of *Little Red Corvette*.

I was looking down Fiona's cleavage where the lavender silk stained her breasts with colour. She saw me looking and grinned. I leant close to her and blew in her ear. 'Fancy making a move soon?'

'Sure.' she said. 'Shall we go and eat?'

'I can think of better things.'

'Later, Sharman,' she said. 'Don't be so impatient. I'm starving.'

'Me too.' But not for food, I thought.

'Where?' she asked.

'How about a Chinese back at my place?'

'You're not getting away that easy.'

'It's late.'

'There'll be something open in Covent.'

'That's what I'm afraid of.'

'Come on, miserable. Treat me to some fancy food and I'll show you a good time.'

'Lawdy, Mizz Scarlett,' I said back, 'you have a tongue like silver.'

She ran her tongue suggestively over her lips. 'And you, sonny, might just get lucky and find out how like silver it is.'

'Come on then,' I said. 'I'm getting a hard on just thinking about it.'

We pulled on our coats and made our various goodbyes, which took me about ten seconds and Fiona about ten minutes, and left the pub.

9

The night outside was sodium bright and getting colder. The breeze was stiffening and the wind chill factor pushing the temperature way down. The streets were beginning to crystallise with ice that caught the reflections of the street lights and kicked them back through 180 degrees until the tarmac appeared to be as polished as a black mirror.

We drove across the river and down Tower Hill and Lower and Upper Thames Street and the Victoria Embankment as far as Blackfriars, then right to High Holborn and left towards Covent Garden. It was perishing cold and the slipstream of the car nearly froze my ears off. But Fiona kept the heater going so that at least our feet were warm.

The streets were lined with parked cars so Fiona drove into a multi-storey NCP on the corner of Endell Street and Shorts Gardens. Even though it was quite late, being the time of year with the festive season almost upon us, the place was still busy. We had to join a queue of cars still trying to get in, and a couple of other cars were waiting behind us when Fiona collected our ticket. There were no free spaces on the lower floors and a little convoy drove to the top floor before we found any room. We parked between an Audi and a VW Beetle that had seen better days.

The pavement was wet from the moisture that filtered down through the porous concrete of the roof and dripped with the beat of a fugue on to the concrete floor. We parked as far from the drips as space would allow. Our feet were noisy on the bare concrete as we followed the illuminated signs that pointed to the lift. There were already four or five people waiting when we got there. It took so long to arrive that I thought it was out of order or switched off, but I heard some movement in the shaft and eventually the single door slid open to reveal an empty cage which stank like all public utility lifts stink.

I shivered as we entered the box. It was getting colder by the minute and the metal walls refrigerated the lift still further. The single stark white bulb recessed into the roof didn't help. One of the geezers in front of us said. 'Ground?' And everyone nodded, and he pushed the button, and the doors shut and the lift dropped, vibrating so much that every ten seconds or so the sides of the cage clipped something in the shaft with a screech that threatened to bring on a stress headache. Eventually, after what seemed like a life sentence, the lift clanged to a halt and the door squealed open. Another foyer, another dim light, another expanse of cold concrete.

We went out into Endell Street and found a bistro about five minutes' walk away. That's what it said over the door: BISTRO, in pink neon on a green background. The sign flashed like a strobe and made me feel giddy. We pushed through a glass door made opaque with condensation, and warm air laced with kitchen smells embraced us.

I could almost see Fiona's mouth start to water. She looked at me and her eyes sparkled. 'Oh, yeah,' she said. 'Let's get to it.'

'Remember your figure.'

She winked. 'Metabolism, Sharman,' she said. 'It's all down to metabolism.'

I felt for my credit cards. As soon as Fiona mentioned metabolism, I knew that Access was in for a caning.

The head waiter, an effete gent in a floor-length white apron, rounded us up like a collie with two recalcitrant sheep. When we asked for a table he checked his watch, looked to the heavens and herded us to a table for two between the kitchen and the Ladies. I pointed to another table, laid for four, quietly situated into a niche in the white-painted walls. He told us it was already set for lunch. I told him we'd eat lunch and made a break for it.

He cut me off like a fullback but he should have concentrated on Fiona. She'd wrong-footed him and was already sitting, coat on the back of a chair, hat and scarf neatly sitting on the next, glomming the menu before he realised he'd been faked out. I took off my coat and neatly folded it over the seat of the third chair at the table and sat down opposite her. He capitulated. His little pigtail bobbed up and down as he inquired: 'Drinks?'

'Martini cocktail,' said Fiona without lifting her head out of the menu.

'Two,' I said.

'Lemon twist or olive?'

'Olive,' I said.

'Lemon,' said Fiona simultaneously.

That was cool. He wouldn't get our drinks mixed up at least. The head waiter split and I picked up my menu. 'What's the recipe today?' I asked.

'Nouvelle, sweetheart, pure nouvelle.'

'Any chips?' I asked.

Our waitress was a chunky American girl wearing a white body shirt and a black skirt, so miniscule as to be almost non-existent. Fiona saw me looking and smacked me with her eyes. Under the white shirt the waitress was wearing a string bra that kept my mind on her measurements and off the prices on the menu which were top of the range and then some.

It was one of those establishments where the staff joined you at the table to discuss the merits of the food. I wasn't fussy but I think Fiona resented the intrusion. The menu was in French and the waitress was from Oklahoma, which caused some confusion, as did the fact that her nipples were erect during the entire conversation.

In retaliation Fiona slid out of her leather jacket like a snake shedding its skin and even the waitress was impressed by her shoulders.

'Sharman, you're scum,' said Fiona when the drinks were in and the waitress had sashayed through the kitchen door, rolling her buttocks as if her behind was chewing a piece of gum. The two guys sitting at a very bad table in the middle of the floor, and making the best of bad job by ostentatiously calling everyone in their address books on a portable telephone, checked the action and started taking their own pulses. Then, when one looked over and saw Fiona's décolletage, he nudged his pal and I swear they called a code and laid back to wait for the crash cart to arrive.

'Naughty,' I said, looking at the lavender silk flowing like water over her breasts. 'The teddy.'

'If I'd known how you'd look at our table person's chest, I'd've worn my old school uniform.'

'It would have worked too.'

'You're a sexist shit.'

'Her bra strap was twisted.'

'Your neck will be twisted, son, if you keep on.'

We clinked glasses and drank. 'I hope you fucking choke,' she whispered as the waitress came back with the first course. I kept my gaze so averted that Fiona almost choked herself.

I don't know exactly what we had ordered but what we got was cold soup, warm duck salad and chocolate pudding. It hadn't sounded like that when the waitress had fluttered her eyelashes at me and taken the order. Serves me right, I suppose. It was OK, not brilliant, but OK. I didn't complain. The company would have made bread and water taste good. With the cocktails, a bottle of wine, two cups of froth without much coffee and six liqueurs, the bill left my credit limit in ashes and we hit the pebbles as warm inside as the night was cold.

When we got back to the car park, it had emptied out and we were alone waiting for the lift. Eventually it arrived and I pushed the button for the top floor. The lift ground and squealed and shimmied its way slowly upwards. The doors opened and we started across the concrete, empty now except for the Spitfire and a green Daimler Sovereign that I remembered had come into the car park immediately after us. I might have been full of food and booze and on a promise and complacent, but I wasn't so complacent that I didn't see the puff of exhaust from the car's idling engine and that there were a number of people inside the car. I stopped short and grabbed Fiona and the two back doors of the Daimler opened as one. The lift doors were just closing behind us and I swung her round and pushed her through the narrowing gap. She shouted something in surprise but I didn't hear what.

'Go down, get help.' I yelled into the lift and a second later I heard the mechanism engage.

I looked round and two men were coming at me fast. Both of them were armed with handguns. I turned again and made for the illuminated sign that said STAIRS and pushed through the fire door. The stairs were concrete with black iron banisters and they were lit as brightly as Runway One at Heathrow. I started down them. I was awkward on my bad leg and the walking stick was no help. I hopped, skipped and jumped down but couldn't get a rhythm going and I broke into a sweat under my clothes.

There were a dozen or so flights between me and the ground floor. I had got down three or four when the door I'd come through at the top of the stairs crashed open. I kept going but looked up and a head popped over the railings above me. I kept going faster. Whoever the hell it was above me fired down into the stairwell. The noise was deafening and a bullet whined off the rail beside me and hit the wall in front of me and went buzzing away down the stairs.

I jumped half the next flight and my leg shot a

bolt of pain right up into my head. Another shot and concrete splintered by my foot. I almost fell down the next flight and I could hear someone running down the stairs above and behind me. I went down the last flight and hit the fire door and I was on the ground floor.

There was no sign of Fiona but the Sovereign screeched down the ramp and skidded to a halt beside me and the back door nearest me opened and a man got out. I backed away and the fire door behind me crashed open and slammed against the wall and I saw who had been shooting at me. He was big and hard looking under a wool worsted suit and I'd never seen him in my life. He was middle aged with hair the same colour as his suit, grey flecked. The one who had got out of the back of the car was younger and slimmer with bushy black hair. He was also wearing a dark suit and I'd never seen him before either. He'd put his gun away but the older man was carrying a Browning model 1935, Hi Power, 9mm Parabellum automatic pistol with an exposed hammer and a thirteen shot clip. No wonder he could afford to waste a few shots down the stairs. He had plenty.

'Sharman, you are fucking dead,' he said, and pulled back the hammer of the gun with his thumb, and my bottle went completely.

Oh shit, oh fuck, no, I thought and moved. I still don't know to this day where I thought I was going. It was goodnight time and the thing I most regretted was that Fiona was involved. The two suits looked as happy as hyenas circling a warm body. The younger one kicked my stick away and I fell on to one knee. Pain shot up my leg and I looked into the muzzle of the automatic. I could almost see the bullet spinning down its cold metal rifling towards my head.

Then the yellow Spitfire came tooling down the ramp far too fast, and instead of braking it accelerated and spun across the greasy concrete towards us with a roar from its engine, a scream from the tyres and a cloud of rubber and exhaust smoke. The little car skidded broadside, and the edge of the front bumper caught the geezer with the gun on the knee.

I heard bone crack like a bread stick breaking amplified a hundred times, and thought that someone else would be limping for a bit. He went down without a sound and lay in a puddle of oil and water with a thin crust of ice around the edges. The liquid began to soak into his jacket. The force of the blow knocked the gun from his hand. It clattered to the floor and slid within my reach.

The young guy went for something under his jacket. I fumbled the gun off the floor and fired without aiming. I hit him in the meat of his right arm and the parabellum bullet chopped a fountain of flesh and blood and material. He screamed and grabbed at the wound with his left hand.

The Spitfire's engine was howling as Fiona rode the accelerator and jockeyed the clutch. I saw the attendant peering out of his booth and then duck down. I pulled myself to my feet and jumped over the top of the passenger door, catching my foot a whack that exploded stars in front of my eyes. I held on to the door frame tight and fought back the tears. The tyres laid rubber as we took off.

I should have shot one of the Daimler's tyres out or blown some glass but I was too shaken up. The barrier was down in front of us and Fiona took it out with the top of the frame of our windscreen and smashed it to matchwood which splintered down around us as we skidded into Endell Street. She almost lost the steering wheel then and the car rocked as the tyres grabbed for traction on the icy road. I felt G-force and turned my head as we sped between parked cars.

As we reached the roundabout and swung left into the eastern end of Longacre, I saw the Daimler hang a fast left behind us with headlights blazing. We lost sight of the car for a second, then it was on our tail as we shot across Drury Lane into Great Queen Street. It stayed with us as we jumped the lights and turned right into Kingsway heading towards The Aldwych and the river beyond.

I clawed myself round to kneel on the passenger seat, feeling the drag of the slipstream, poked the gun over the back of the car and fired. I got off two shots that went nowhere before the gun jammed. I slammed the weapon hard on the metalwork of the car, something that is not recommended by gun freaks, and pointed the weapon back again and pulled the trigger. The gun kicked and the right headlamp of the Daimler blew out. I fired again and the bullet knocked sparks off the bonnet of the car. I squeezed the trigger once more and a third bullet spanged off the bumper. There were just a few pedestrians about and they probably thought we were making a film. The driver of the Daimler and I knew it was only a matter of time before I did serious damage. He dropped right back as we tore into the Strand and pulled over to go back into The Aldwych as we drove on to Waterloo Bridge.

'Slow down,' I screamed into Fiona's ear, and she did so. I tossed the gun over the parapet of the bridge from the car as we were still moving and sat trying to hold myself together as the lights of Waterloo Station came up very fast in front of us.

10

We passed the station on our right and turned into Bayliss Road at the traffic lights. The only witnesses were some dossers taking comfort from the all-night coffee stall under the railway bridge. They were too busy dreaming of their long-lost mothers and the heat from the cardboard that they burnt under the arches to keep themselves alive to bother with us.

Then Fiona lost us in a warren of Dickensian squares backed up to black brick warehouses with high, barred windows that slashed our headlights back at us. The squares were connected by narrow back alleys, double yellow-banded, still hung with gas lights, where you could shake off a Siamese twin, the turns and bends were so sharp and tortuous.

We approached the estate where she lived from the Oval end and she swung round to her lock-up. We hid the car and ourselves away from prying eyes behind double-locked doors.

We climbed out of the car and Fiona spoke for the first time. 'I don't believe that happened. Not for real.'

'Why didn't you go downstairs like I said?'

'I didn't know what was going on. I went down

one level and back up the ramp. I saw the car that chased us going down and then I heard shots and I went and got my car.'

'You could have been killed.'

'You *would* have been killed.'

She was right. 'Thank Christ you did,' I said. 'Come here.'

I held her tightly and she dug her fingernails into my arms. 'Oh, Nick. My God, what have I done?'

'You saved my life,' I said. 'Simple as that.'

She went a bit green then under the fluorescent tube that lit the inside of her garage and I held her more tightly. 'All right. I'm all right,' she said.

'I owe you one.' Several, I thought.

'Not between us, no debts,' she replied. And we didn't have to say any more.

We picked our way through the broken glass and empty beer cans and dog shit to the entrance to the flats, and pretty soon we were heading upwards. I thought of all the lifts in the world that stank like toilets, and how far away and yet so close they were to neon signs that wrote BISTRO across the night, and the cold soup and warm duck salad and chocolate pudding tasted sour in the back of my throat.

We went through the security locks into her flat and bolted the door behind us. I went to the kitchen and found a litre of vodka and took a hit straight from the bottle. Fiona looked at me. I offered her a drink and she shook her head. I drank some more and the spirit was oily in my mouth and burnt my throat right down to my gut but didn't warm me.

Fiona took me by the hand and led me into the

living room. I followed silently, still carrying the bottle. The room was shadowy, lit only by the hall light reflected through the half-open door.

'Make love to me,' she whispered, all throaty and shivery. 'Here, now.'

And the way she said it turned me on, so I did. Half on and half off the oatmeal-coloured sofa, both of us half dressed. I pushed her skirt up and tore at the thin piece of silk that barely covered her crotch. The two buttons that fastened it between her legs flew off and fell God knows where and her pubis was exposed, all wet and tangled under my hands. And when I entered her, her cunt was like a hot swamp. But I couldn't come because as we slammed against each other I thought of what had happened and how close it had been. Each time I got near I heard the sound of the assassin's leg breaking, and I lost it. She came once quickly, and then again, but all I got was sore and frustrated while my mind jumped around like a cat on a hotplate. Afterwards we went upstairs to bed but I couldn't sleep. I kept thinking I was back in trouble, bad trouble, and this time Fiona was all the way in it with me.

She went out like she had dropped off a cliff. I lay next to her for half an hour, smoking, then got up, pulled on a pair of jeans and went back to the vodka for comfort.

I walked around the flat, going from one window to another, looking out over London. Everywhere lights gleamed like jewels but on the streets themselves I knew it was cold and dirty. I heard the sound of sirens all night long, some close, some far away. They moaned and screamed, and I imagined that they were searching for me on the hard black-top. But I knew there were plenty of other clients of tragedy. People who were robbing and killing each other and burning down their own houses like rats made crazy on a treadmill.

I looked up and there were blood spots on the moon. I watched it quarter the clear sky and the stars went out one by one as the dawn approached.

We made the four o'clock and five o'clock and six o'clock news on LBC. 'An incident', it said. No busted up bodies lying in pools of ice water, no yellow Spitfire or gunshots. Just 'an incident' made ordinary by the tone of the news reader's voice, and I looked at my hands in the moonlight and they seemed to be as spotted with blood as the moon itself and shook like they had a life of their own.

Around seven I went into Fiona's bathroom cabinet. It was like a mini Boots the Chemist. She visited dodgy quacks in Harley Street about once a month and for a tenner or so got enough scrips to paper the walls. I found a bottle of Duromine half full of shiny turquoise and grey capsules. They were each equivalent to about a quarter of a bomber, so I swallowed three. I was going to have to be alert for the day but I didn't want to be wired so I took a few DF 118s to buffer the speed and rolled a joint of DP and mixed some vodka with orange juice for vitamin C and natural goodness and to wash down the pills. By the time I woke Fiona at eight, I was a different man.

'Shit,' she said, when I stuck a cup of black coffee under her nose. 'I had a terrible dream.'

Then she saw my face and realisation dawned. 'It wasn't a dream, was it?'

I shook my head and saw tears fill her eyes. 'Keep it together, sweetheart,' I said. 'Don't go on me now. You saved our lives. You did right. They wouldn't be crying over us this morning.' I squeezed her shoulder. 'You were great.'

'It was so unreal.'

'Real enough that we're on the news.'

'What?'

'Relax, no names, no car reg, nothing to tie us in.' She fell back on to her pillow and the coffee slopped over the side of the mug.

'I got that bastard good and proper, didn't I?' she said, and grinned, and I knew she was all right. South London girls – I fucking love 'em.

'What are you doing today?' I asked.

'Nothing much.'

'Good, I'm going to need a chauffeur. We've got places to go, people to see.'

'Who? Where?'

'I'm not sure yet, but I'll know the places when we get there and the people when I see them. Now get up, shower, dress, and let's go.'

11

Fiona put on Chinos and a leather jacket. I wore similar. We looked like we were going out on a bombing raid over Berlin.

'Got any tools in that garage of yours?' I asked.

'Like what?'

'Screwdrivers, spanners.'

'Yeah, why?'

'I'm going to get you a new set of number plates for your car.'

'Where from?'

'It's a V-reg, isn't it?'

'Yes.'

'From any V-reg car we can find in a quiet spot.'

'Swop them?' she asked.

'Steal them. We'll keep yours.'

'But I thought you said there was nothing about the car on the news?'

'So I did. But that doesn't mean the boys in blue don't have the number. The attendant in the garage could've got it as we drove out, and it doesn't hurt to have a spare set of plates, just in case.'

'If you say so.'

We went down to the garage and got the car and cruised the streets for a bit. I spotted a

V-registered Granada Ghia parked up an alley behind a launderette and had the plates off in less than two minutes. We drove to a back street in Brixton and with a Phillips screwdriver I punched extra holes in the plates and tore a fingernail getting the registration off the Spitfire, then fitted the new plates neatly into place and hid the originals under the carpet in the boot.

'Can't do much about the colour,' I said. 'We'll just have to live with it.'

I got Fiona to drive me to my office. The telephone was ringing when we arrived. I hitched myself up on the edge of the desk and picked up the receiver. It was cold in the room and Fiona lit the gas fire. 'Sharman,' I said.

'Teddy.'

'Hi, Teddy. What's cooking?'

'Not a lot my end. Uncle's in front of the beak this afternoon. I'm going down.'

'I need to see you first.'

'Why?'

'Someone tried to kill me last night.'

'Straight?'

'It's on the news.'

'Christ, what happened?'

'They didn't succeed,' I said dryly.

'Obviously.'

'Where are you?' I asked.

'At home.' He didn't elaborate.

'Give me a clue, where's that, Teddy?'

'Peckham.'

'A lovely spot.'

'Get off my case, man.'

'Hey, don't talk about cases. You're speaking to

someone who was almost brown bread last night.
And it wouldn't just have been me.'

'Who else?'

'The woman I was with.'

'Yeah, man,' he said slowly. 'Sorry. Forget I said
it.'

'Right. Now it doesn't take great deduction to
work out that it probably had something to do with
Emerald's little problem. I knew I should have nished
the whole deal.'

'But you didn't.'

'And now I think I need to see Mr Lupino, and
sharpish.'

'You reckon he was behind it?'

'How the hell do I know? But if he was, it's worth
letting him know I don't frighten that easy.' Frighten,
who was I kidding? 'And I'm not on intimate terms
with the gentleman. Your little firm obviously is.'

'What do you want me to do?'

'Cancel seeing Em. Come here instead.'

'Where's here?'

'My office.' I told him where it was.

'And?' he asked.

'Do you know how to get through to Lupino?'

'I've got a number.'

'Bring it.'

'I'll be with you in an hour.'

'I'll be here.'

'Bye,' he said and hung up.

I picked up the receiver again and rang
Endesleigh. He was in court, due back after lunch. I
left my name but no message and put the receiver
down. The telephone rang again immediately.

'Sharman,' I said again.

'Mister Dark wants to see you.' The voice was hoarse and Cockney and didn't fill me with bonhomie. Just the way he chose his words pissed me off.

'Who?' I asked.

'Jack Dark,' the voice replied.

I said not a word, just stayed with the telephone receiver getting warm in my hand and looked at Fiona still sitting by the fire. She looked up and smiled, although it seemed a little forced. I winked back.

'Are you there?' the voice asked after a moment. Its tone was hoarser and the accent harder as though the speaker was used to people he called up paying strict attention to his wishes, if not being so terrified that they just babbled away in overdrive. I wasn't impressed.

'Yes, I'm here,' I said, and wished I was somewhere else.

'Did you hear what I said?'

'I did.'

'And?'

'And nothing. I don't want to see Jack Dark, whoever he is, and don't bother to give me any cryptic clues until I fall in. I guarantee I won't.'

'Mister Dark is a very important man.'

'That's purely subjective,' I said.

'Do what?'

'Who or what's important to one person, in other words you, may be of sublime disinterest to another person, in other words me.'

'Well, that's as maybe, but he wants to see you, and if he wants something he usually gets it.'

'If that's right, then he's a lucky man.'

'That is right, and he is, very lucky.'

'I think his luck just ran out,' I said. 'I've got other fish to fry. I think I'll pass.'

'Don't get fucking funny with me! That's not the way it works and you know it. Mister Dark wants you to meet him tonight at twelve-thirty outside Aldwych tube.'

'Shall I bring my membership card?' I asked.

'What membership card?'

'My membership card to the Black Hand Gang. Now don't you get fucking funny! I don't meet strange men after midnight in the street. I'm not that kind of girl. And, besides, there's altogether too many people want me out of the way for me to engage in that old malarky. So tell Mister Dark, thanks, but no thanks.'

'All right, mate,' said the voice. 'Have it your way. We'll be in touch.' And he put the phone down.

I looked at the receiver, dead in my hand, and replaced it carefully on the hook.

'Who was that?' asked Fiona.

'Someone called Jack Dark wants to see me.'

'Who's Jack Dark?' she asked.

'Dunno. Does the name mean anything to you?'

She pulled a face and shrugged. 'Not a thing.'

'Nor me.' I said. 'But he knows me, and like I said he wants to see me.'

'What about?'

'Who knows? I declined the offer.'

'Do you think . . . ?'

I shivered as the speed took hold. 'I've given up thinking for Lent.'

Fiona made coffee while we waited for Teddy. It

---

was wet and warm which was the most that could be said for it.

He arrived about ten-thirty in the BMW. He was wearing a pale grey, double-breasted suit, white shirt, discreetly patterned tie and shiny black brogues. We watched him through the plate glass front of my office as he walked from the car.

'Superfly,' I said.

'Hunky,' said Fiona.

Fine, I thought, that's all I need.

He pushed open the office door, posed in the doorway for a second and came in. 'Nice place,' he said.

'Thanks, Teddy.'

He looked round. 'Could do with a lick of paint here and there.'

'Shall we talk interior design another time?' I said. 'Meet Fiona, a very good friend of mine.' I emphasised the 'good'.

'Charmed,' said Teddy.

'Me too,' said Fiona, and looked it.

Introductions over, I got straight down to the nitty. 'Lupino,' I said. 'You say you've got a number for him?'

'Yes.'

'How come? Where did you get it from?'

Teddy looked at me and went over to where the telephone directories were stacked on a shelf behind my desk. He pulled out the Business & Services book and dropped it in front of me.

'Under "L",' he said. 'Where you could have found it. I thought you were supposed to be a detective.'

I felt like a berk.

I shrugged and thumbed through the pages and sure enough there it was: Lupino Fruit and Veg. Wholesalers, with an address in Nine Elms. 'You could have told me that on the phone,' I said.

'And miss the look on your face? No way.'

I pulled over the telephone and dialled the number listed. It rang once. 'Lupino's Fruit and Veg,' said a woman's voice.

'Mr Lupino please.'

'I'll see if he's available. Who's calling?'

'Nick Sharman.'

The phone clicked and started playing the main theme from *Chariots of Fire* in my ear.

I looked at Teddy as I waited. The music stopped and the telephone clicked again. 'What?' said a man's voice.

'Bimpson Lupino. I'd like to talk to him.'

'You and thousands, mate. What's it about?'

'I think he probably knows.'

'Are we playing guessing games or what?'

'Tell him it's about Emerald.'

'So?'

'Does he know where Emerald is?'

'Yes.'

So we *were* playing guessing games. 'Does he know what happened to me last night?'

'He knows a lot of things.'

'Then tell him I've already slipped his name in the frame, and if anything happens to me or mine he's likely to get a little visit.'

'You are a silly cunt, aren't you?' asked the voice, and the phone went down with a bang. No songs from the shows that time. I waited for two or three minutes. 'You're in luck,' said the voice eventually. 'Mister Lupino will see you tonight at the Royal Hotel in Bickley. Go through the town on the London Road and it's on the right, set back from the road, all lit up. You can't miss it. The Guv'nor will be in the Vegas Bar. It's a private party for the firm, so mind your manners. Be there at nine-thirty. The dinner will be over and the dancing will have begun. Ask for Mister Lupino's party, and come alone. Understood?'

'Yes,' I said and the speaker hung up.

I put the phone down. 'Tonight, Bickley, alone.'

'Bollocks,' said Fiona. 'I'm going with you. I'm in this as much as you. Do you expect me just to go home and wash out a few pairs of knickers while you have all the fun?'

Fun! I thought. Jesus!

'Besides, I'm your driver.'

'I can drive,' I said. 'It's about time I gave the motor a spin.'

'I'll drive you,' interrupted Teddy. 'Uncle said I was to help.'

I sat and chewed the inside of my mouth as the speed surged through me. 'What the hell?' I said. 'We'll *all* go to the ball.'

12

About then I thought it was time for a livener. We took both cars up to the wine bar where Teddy and I had eaten lunch the previous day. It seemed like a thousand years ago.

This morning there was a camp boy behind the bar doing the frug to some old *Martha and the Vandellas* number blasting out of the stereo. The bar was empty and he stopped dancing and turned down the volume as we came in. Teddy and Fiona went to a table and I went to get the drinks in.

'Hello,' said the boy. 'What can I get you?'

'Three Rocks, please.'

He went to the fridge.

'I haven't seen you for a bit,' I said to make conversation and stop myself gnawing at my tongue.

'I've been on holiday.'

'Do anything good?'

'I had my nipples pierced.'

There is absolutely no answer to that. 'Really?' I managed to say.

'Yes.'

'Was it painful?'

'Excruciating,' he said as he opened the bottles and put them, and three glasses on the bar top. 'But it was worth it.' He leant closer and lowered his voice as I rescued a fiver from my back pocket. 'I've got nipple rings in them, and my lover attaches a gold chain and leads me around the house at night.'

'Makes my sex life look positively dull,' I said.

He looked over at Teddy and Fiona and raised an eyebrow. 'I'd say it had definite possibilities myself.'

I looked too. 'Fine,' I said. 'Catch you later.' And I took the beers over.

I told Teddy and Fiona about the party in Bickley, and that I'd told Endesleigh about Bim. I didn't tell them what his reaction had been. I asked Teddy about Jack Dark but he'd never heard of him. We had a couple of beers and I gave Teddy my address and arranged for him to pick us up from there at eight. Fiona wanted to go home and get her best party frock. I volunteered to go with her but she declined the offer. She told me to go to my own home and get some sleep. Fat chance. I explained I was worried about her going off alone after the previous night's excitement, and she told me firmly that she wasn't going to change her life because of some cheap crooks. In the end I gave in. Around two we left the bar and Fiona dropped me at home and sped off.

The envelope was waiting on the mat when I opened the street door. It was thick and unstamped with just my name scrawled on the front in felt tip pen. I leant against the wall and tore the flap open. Inside was a wodge of the dirtiest banknotes I'd ever seen. I riffled the pile. It was a lot. I took the money and myself up to my flat, popped open a bottle of Rock, lit a cigarette and counted the cash.

When I finished I discovered I was five thousand pounds richer and my hands were five thousand pounds grubbier. The money was in fifties, twenties and tens. The cash wasn't sorted, so I sorted it myself. I'm neat that way.

I put the money back in the envelope and threw it on top of the draining board. I washed my hands in the kitchen sink, dried them on a tea towel, finished the beer, threw the bottle in the garbage and lit another Silk Cut. I walked around the flat thinking. I called Fiona. She had just got home and all was quiet. I didn't tell her about the money. Then I telephoned Endesleigh again. He was at his desk.

'Sharman,' I said.

'I'm honoured, three times in two days. What's up?'

I told him.

'And you just left the scene?'

'What was I supposed to do? Take notes. They were going to kill us.'

He said nothing in reply.

'What happened to the pair that went down?' I asked after a bit.

'The one you shot dragged the other into the car and they took off after you.'

'They didn't catch me. Did you catch them?'

'No. What happened to the gun?'

'I deep sixed it off Waterloo bridge.'

'Very good. The charges are many and various.'

'Come on, man. I didn't have to tell you. And I didn't start it. It was self-defence. Someone's after me, the same day as I tell you about Em and Bim. Now do you believe me?'

'What's Lupino got to do with it?'

'Oh, come on. He knew about it. I spoke to one of his lackeys.'

'Prove it. Lupino knows about a lot.'

'That's what his lackey said.'

'Look, Sharman,' said Endesleigh, 'your past goes back a long way. Maybe a piece of it caught up with you last night.'

'Yeah, maybe.'

'Come in and talk to me about it sometime. Sometime soon.'

'Got the bracelets ready?'

'I don't think it'll come to that.'

'OK. I'll be in.'

'Don't forget. I'd hate to have to get someone to come and collect you.'

'I won't. Anything about Emerald?'

'He'll be on remand. He's safe. Don't worry, if I get any news you'll be the first to know.'

'Thanks. One last thing.'

'What?' he sighed.

'Someone name of Jack Dark. Know him?'

'Not that I know of.'

'Check out the name for me, will you?'

'Why?'

'Just interested.'

'Do you think this is an information bureau?'

'No, but as a favour.'

'One of too many.'

'You're a diamond,' I said. 'I'll be in. See you.' And I hung up. I didn't tell him about the five grand either.

I took the bag of money and put it in my sock drawer, lit another cigarette and sat back in my easy chair with my feet on the coffee table.

At five the telephone rang. I guessed who it would be and I was right. The same hoarse, Cockney voice was on the line. 'Did you get it?' he asked.

There were jokes aplenty there but I was trying to give them up. 'What?' I asked innocently.

'The dough.'

'I got it,' I said. 'But I don't want it.'

'It's yours, mate. Mister Dark sent it.'

'So I guessed.'

'And he still wants to see you. It's a gesture of good faith.'

That kind of faith I could handle. I had to admit I was intrigued. Five grand's worth. 'He's persistent,' I said.

'I told you, didn't I? He says you're right to be cautious and not make a meet in the open. Will a restaurant do?'

'Doesn't he speak himself, or is he too exclusive?'

'He speaks all right, you'll find out, so is a restaurant OK?'

'What restaurant?'

'The Mogul Empire in Gray's Inn Road. Do you know it?'

'I dare say I could find it.'

'Mister Dark has an Indian every Saturday night. He's asked you to see him there tomorrow.'

'What time?'

'About ten.'

'How will I know him?' I asked.

'Just ask for Mister Dark's table. So shall I tell him you'll be there?'

'Unless something more interesting comes up,' I said, and put down the receiver.

He didn't phone back.

13

I changed into a clean white shirt, dark suit and tie, and sat around the flat in the dark watching TV with the sound turned down, chewing on my lips and feeling as jittery as a used car salesman going for a polygraph test. The flat bell rang just before eight. I got up and went over and moved the curtain and saw Teddy standing on the forecourt of the house. I rapped on the glass and he looked up. I went down to meet him and took my coat and stick because I didn't want to walk upstairs again.

When I opened the front door, he was standing in the porch. 'All right, Teddy?' I said.

'Fine.'

'How's Uncle?'

'Not so good, refused bail, and he's being moved to Brixton.'

'I hope they've counted his arms and legs.'

'Don't worry, they have.'

'He'll be cool, man,' I said. 'We'll get him out.'

I saw Teddy's teeth flash in a grin. 'Sure we will.'

I looked for the BMW. 'Where's the car?'

'There.' And he pointed to the vehicle that was blocking the driveway. It was a new-looking Suzuki SJ413 with a soft top. Under the harsh white light

119

from the street lamps I saw that the Japanese jeep was turquoise and lavender with a white hood. It looked like an exotic variety of ice-cream. I shut the house door behind me, pulled on my coat against the cold night air and walked over and tried the passenger door. It was unlocked.

I opened it and climbed warily into the seat, scanning the interior. Cellphone, CD player and a radio that did everything bar make the tea. I suppose the car had less gadgets than the flight deck of a space shuttle, but it was a close call. Teddy, who had followed me over, opened the driver's door, got behind the wheel and switched on the sidelights. The dash lit up like the New York skyline.

'No wonder you guys exchanged a whole continent for a handful of beads and mirrors,' I said.

'Have you ever been punched in the mouth?' asked Teddy, in a not unfriendly way.

'Often. But Emerald told you to help me, not inflict actual bodily harm. I suppose you wear colour co-ordinated boxer shorts.'

'Your jokes are crap and you never let up.'

'That's what my wife used to say.'

'I didn't know you were married.'

'I'm not.'

'See what I mean.'

'Are you?' I asked to make conversation.

'Shit, no, man. I don't need that kind of piano on my back. I like to spread myself thin. There's too much of me for just one woman.'

'Oh, Jesus,' I said. 'Joe Cool.'

His teeth flashed in the half darkness. 'That's my name, baby, don't wear it out.' Teddy seemed in high good humour which was more than I could say for myself.

'So where is the lady?' he asked.

'She'll be here,' I said, and as if to prove me right the little yellow car barrelled up the road towards us and slid to a halt on the other side of the street with a squeal of rubber. Fiona killed the engine and the lights and opened her door and climbed out. I opened the door of the jeep and called to her.

'Christ, is that you?' she said. 'What's this, something out of a Christmas cracker?'

'Funny,' said Teddy.

I got out of the jeep and pulled the front seat forward on its hinges. 'Get in,' I said.

Fiona climbed into the back seat. I hitched myself in and looked at her. She was all wrapped up in a dark coat and had a man's trilby pulled down over her hair. 'What's the story?' she asked.

'No change. We go to the hotel, you two find somewhere out of the way. I go and see Lupino and suss him out. Don't forget, I was told to come alone. If it's cool, I come and get you. If not, I don't.'

'What about me?' asked Teddy.

'You're a different matter. I believe you said that Bim and his buddies are not partial to people of your particular ethnic persuasion.'

'So?'

'So, you're staying out of that room.'

'I thought I might be.'

'Back of the bus job,' I said. 'Sorry.'

'Don't worry, I've had that every day of my life.'

And I suppose he had. No wonder he wasn't mad about whites. I left it. What more could I say?

Teddy ground the starter of the jeep and the

engine caught first time. He switched the lights to full beam, slid the stubby gearstick into first, checked over his shoulder and pulled out into the street. We went back to the South Circular where I seemed to be spending half my life lately and down through the 'burbs to Bickley and all the delights it had to offer.

The main roads were like bandages of light stretched across a wounded city. They were soda-pop orange striped with neon red and blue and sickly green that turned the pedestrians' faces corpselike. As the highways were light so the back streets and alleyways were dark. So dark indeed that they stole the memory of light from the street lamps spaced too far apart and the odd unshaded window and ground it flat into the gutters.

It was mini-cab city where we were going. Black cabbies seem to think you need a visa to get into New Cross and Peckham. So every other car we saw seemed to be a four door coke-bottle Cortina with a thin, chrome, magnetic aerial resting on a piece of plastic to save the re-spray.

There were a lot of rusty white Transits too, being driven by fat geezers in T-shirts who either couldn't afford jumpers or thought it was the height of machismo to freeze their upper arms in the December frost. Teddy drove well. He put a Marvin Gaye CD into the machine and we listened and hardly spoke as we went.

We got to the outskirts of Bickley about nine and drove through the town as directed. The entrance to the Royal Hotel loomed up on our right just as the voice on the telephone had promised. The front of the building was lit up to match the Christmas tree set on the lawn in front of the main door to the hotel. The place had all the signs. A tasty little crib for villains to cut the mustard. Straights also served as camouflage, of course. Teddy followed the signs to the car park. I'd gone right off them after my last little excursion and told him so. He told me to relax and drove to the farthest corner, away from the lights and at least thirty feet from the nearest motor. Right then I wished I hadn't thrown the Browning in the river.

14

We got out of the car and walked across the blacktop and around the front to the revolving doors of the hotel.

Inside it was party time for the local swingers. All the crims in South London who had made good and migrated down the Old Kent Road until they hit enough green to call the country and had settled down and taken root. The place was chocka with the nouveaux riches. I had spotted Rollers and Porsches and Bentleys and big BMWs and the odd Cadillac and Stingray in the car park.

There were a lot of young tarts about hanging on to older men with hair clawed over their bare scalps and a tendency to paunchiness. And old tarts too with their toy boys. The place was full of hungry-eyed females. I know I'm no Richard Gere but I could feel their eyes crawling over me at forty feet. I tell you what, if you couldn't pull in the Royal Hotel, Bickley, you might as well collect your P45 and apply for your pension. Of course, if you did pull you could just offend some face and might well end up under the foundations of the M2 extension as between the sheets with a mystery for a night of passion. Fiona noticed the looks too and flashed me one of her own. I was pleased that Teddy got more than me.

We crossed the overheated foyer to the check-in desk and I beckoned the receptionist over. He was a fat old queen in a tight grey suit. 'Vegas Bar?' I queried.

'Through the doors there.' He pointed. 'Into the Lloyd-Webber wing.' I was beginning to get the taste of the place by then.

'But there's a private party on tonight,' he added.

'I'm expected,' I said. 'Is there another bar?'

'Of course, sir, several. The Cocktail Bar, the Lounge Bar and the Jolly Cockney Bar.'

We were spoilt for choice. 'Not the Jolly Cockney Bar,' said Fiona.

'Where's the Lounge Bar?' I asked.

'Just across the foyer, sir, and down one flight of stairs.' He pointed again.

'Thanks.'

'My pleasure.'

'You want to wait for me in there?' I said to Teddy and Fiona.

'Looks like we don't have much choice,' she said back.

I didn't argue, just made kissy face at her, waved and went in the direction the receptionist had indicated, through double doors and along a thickly carpeted corridor decorated with pictures of Old Bickley, and then to another set made of polished wood and sparkling crystal, etched with motifs of flowers and grapes. A board had been set up in front of the doors. In white plastic lettering on a black background it read:

VEGAS BAR CLOSED
PRIVATE PARTY

'Mister Lupino,' I said to the maître d' who was guarding the door against all comers as if his life depended on it, which it probably did. 'He's expecting me. My name is Sharman.'

The maître d' beckoned over a white-jacketed waiter, whispered in his ear and sent him scuttling over to a gangster in a powder blue tux with matching frills on his dress shirt. He, in his turn, threaded his way through the crowd up a couple of wide stairs to a quieter part of the bar and spoke to half a ton of swarthy trouble shoe-horned into a Moss Bros reject that fitted as tightly as a condom. The huge guy looked over at me and then turned and vanished into the gloom. I was left standing.

Then the story reversed itself. The big bloke came back and spoke to the powder blue tux who hurried down the stairs and spoke to the waiter who was still waiting. Which was his job, after all. The waiter came back to the maître d' and whispered for half a minute to him. The maître d' squinted down his nose at me, which was difficult as I was at least three inches taller than he was, and said in a cod French accent, 'Monsieur Lupino will see you now.'

'Cheers,' I said bravely back with no accent at all, and slid around him into the bar like Daniel into the lion's den. It was packed inside and the air-conditioning was taking a hiding. The bar was awash with Christmas. Any more tinsel and the rafters would have collapsed. The room was full of bimbos getting near the end of their shelf life and clutching on to their sexuality with sharp red nails and the help of sun beds and designer dresses in suede and Lurex.

There was a four-piece combo on a dais in the

corner farthest from the bar, playing a turgid version of *You've Got A Friend*. The wives, with their silver tints and panda white eyes and third finger left hand crusted with diamonds, were envying their own daughters' youthfulness and mouthing the words of the song to their disinterested husbands, as if it would bring some excitement back into their marriages.

Fat chance.

I made my way through the crowd and the band segued into *Billie Jean* and I was up the broad steps into the sanctum.

The festivities hadn't percolated across to this corner of the bar. Even the decorations looked sad. There were four men standing where maybe a dozen would fit comfortably. But no one was interested in intruding on their personal space. The bar top was littered with empty glasses rimed with scum. The minder was waiting for me with two regulation well-hard razor boys whose tailors allowed an extra inch or so in their jackets on the opposite side to their gun hand to allow room for a shoulder holster. The fourth man was different. I could tell that even though he was standing back out of the dim light that filtered through from where the main action was.

I stood for a minute.

The huge man came over to me. 'Sharman?' he asked.

I nodded. He sounded like whoever I'd spoken to when I'd telephoned Nine Elms earlier.

The heavy shook his head. More in sorrow than in anger, I think. 'You fucking mug,' he said, and went over to the fourth man. He stood with his back towards the bar, facing out across the dance floor with a perfect view of all the room. A sniper's view.

The heavy went and whispered in his ear. The whole crew must have had videos of *The Godfather* at home.

I saw a glint from Bimpson Lupino's eyes and he motioned for me to step forward into his presence.

'Mister Lupino,' I said.

He was taller than I had expected, better looking, better dressed. I'd expected Edward G. Robinson and I got Anthony Quinn playing Aristotle Onassis in a crappy mini series. He stuck out his hand and I shook it. I only counted my fingers once when I got it back.

'Mister Sharman, so glad you could come,' he said. 'I've heard a lot about you.'

Unfortunately his voice let him down. It was thick and ugly. Half Cockney and half Greek, but no jokes about kebabs. He had nice teeth though and he knew it. He left them uncovered too long after every smile.

He pointed to the heavy. 'Max,' he said. Max nodded as if it hurt. I nodded back. The razor boys were Rick and Lonzo. More nods, more pain. 'You want a booze?' Bim asked.

'Lovely,' I said calmly, but I was shitting myself. I felt like a fillet steak in a pool full of piranha fish.

Lonzo rapped on top of the bar and a rabbity girl in a white blouse and black skirt popped up like a jack in the box. Although the rest of the bar was packed and people were cutting each other's throats for a drink, it seemed that Mister Lupino was not to be kept waiting.

'Same again,' said Lonzo. 'And?' He looked at me.

'Vodka and tonic,' I said. 'Large one.'

Lonzo squinted at me, but ordered the drink nevertheless. I was glad to see the barmaid free pour from a Blue Label bottle.

I picked my drink off the bar. I was shaking but it was controllable. I liked that. It made me feel better. Rick bumped me and nearly made me spill my drink. 'You got heat?' he asked.

'What, like a Calor gas stove?'

'You think you're funny, don't you?'

'Yeah,' I said back. 'Sometimes I wake up in the middle of the night just laughing all over my face.'

'You see how funny it is when I put that stick up your arse.'

'You can try, if that's what turns you on, sweets,' I said. 'But I wouldn't recommend it.'

I hoped I sounded tougher than I felt.

'Knock it off, the pair of you,' said Lupino.

I was willing but Rick wasn't. 'You stub your toe in the shower?' he asked spitefully.

I was getting tired of him and so was his boss. 'Rick, I said knock it off, I won't tell you again,' he said.

'Do what the man says or Santa won't pop down your chimney next week,' I said.

'And you,' said Lupino.

Rick and I both glared at each other and retired from the fray unhurt.

The drugs and booze were beginning to screw up my peripheral vision. I kept seeing hallucinations out of the corners of my eyes. They say when you stop taking it, it gets worse. My advice, don't stop.

One of the hallucinations was sitting on a bar stool at the bottom of the short flight of steps. I hadn't noticed her on my way in. I'd been too busy trying to walk forwards and watch my back at the same time. She was short, that was obvious. Her feet dangled at least nine inches off the deep red carpet and twined around the metal pole that supported the seat. She was white-skinned and bottle blonde, and the bottle was fighting a losing battle with the darkness of her body hair. So dark in fact that I could see a faint suggestion of a moustache on her top lip. Her hair was a yellow fuzz, dry and static-filled. She was big, broad-shouldered but soft. Her hundred and forty pounds was stuffed into a raspberry pink satin frock, so tight that the material was threatening to call time out at several pressure points along the side seams. The colour and cut of her dress flattered neither complexion nor figure. She was sipping at a cocktail whose colour exactly matched the shade of her frock. Her dumpy legs were encased in black fish net and the flesh bulged through the mesh like warm lard. I imagined the cellulite marching up the backs of her legs like footsteps in the snow.

Bim saw me looking. 'My youngest daughter, Antonia,' he said.

I stopped thinking bad thoughts in case mind reading was one of his many talents and tried to look admiring.

'A picture, Mister Lupino.'

He looked at me closely to see if I was taking the

piss. 'A good girl,' he said. 'But she needs a husband.'

The good girl's face was like urban blight made flesh. I don't know why she hadn't taken advantage of Daddy's cash and visited a discreet private clinic for some cosmetic surgery. Perhaps the old man thought she was cute. Perhaps a surgeon wouldn't know where to start.

She drained her glass and cracked the counter with the stem. A barman came at the double carrying a jug full of the same pink mess and topped up her glass. She sneered at him and he blanched and backed away. She looked like she was a right chip off the old block. She pulled a cigarette from the packet on the bar in front of her and waved it about, and two handsome boys appeared, one on each side of her, and fought over who would fire it up. The look she gave them nearly took their ears off.

'She seems to have plenty of admirers here,' I remarked.

'I pay them fuckers to be attentive,' said Bim.

'Is your good lady wife here tonight?' I asked in a friendly manner. Bim pointed with his eyes and I looked over the heads of the revellers to where a pudden in glacé blue was dancing with an adolescent boy a clear two feet taller than she was. He was bending over her like a flamingo catching shrimp and looking about as pink around the earholes.

'My old woman and my nephew Ben.'

'They make a handsome couple.'

Now he knew I was taking the rise and his eyes narrowed. I decided to leave family matters well alone. I sipped at my glass and Bim said, 'Glad as I am to meet you at last, it could have been under better circumstances.'

'You can say that again!'

'I believe you've even mentioned my name to the police?'

'They've heard it before,' I said.

He gave me a look that could have frozen blood. 'Why did you think it necessary to jog their memories?'

'I think you know.'

He shook his head.

'I think you do,' I said.

'What makes you think that?'

'Last night, Covent Garden, three men in a green Daimler. Armed men. One was about to shoot me and probably the girl I was with. If it hadn't been for her, we'd both be dead now.'

'I still don't know how that involves me.'

'She ran one down, I shot another, and we frightened the driver off. Does that jog your memory?'

'You're crazy, boy, if you think I had anything to do with that.'

'But you do know about it?'

He did the continental walk and hummed and hawed with his hands. He knew all right. 'I know lots of things,' he said.

'Everybody tells me that,' I said.

I finished my drink and tapped for another one without waiting to be asked.

'So?' he said when the barmaid had topped up my glass.

'So it's going to make Old Bill a bit suspicious. I

go in telling them that someone has stitched up Emerald, I mention your name, and the same day someone tries to kill me. It might make them look a little deeper into the job that was done on Emerald.'

'They can look twice at anything they like as far as I'm concerned. I repeat, I had nothing to do with Watkins's trouble. If he wishes to deal drugs that is his affair. If he gets caught it's his own fault. You are looking for a scapegoat and you chose me. I do not appreciate my name being bandied about police stations. I think I may have to teach you a lesson.'

I saw the razor boys tensing for action. Lupino really was behind the times.

'Leave me alone,' I said. 'There's people here who are expecting me to join them for a drink later, in one piece. They know where I am and who I'm with and if I turn up half dead in some back alley or just disappear they'll scream "Police" so loud not even you will be able to shut them up. And another thing, if you do decide to teach me a lesson, make it a permanent one, because if I'm alive I'll grass you up and enjoy every minute of it. If I mentioned your name, so what? If you're innocent you've got nothing to worry about. Someone tried to mark my card last night, in permanent ink. I want it stopped.'

Bimpson's fists were opening and closing in anger.

'You brought someone?' he said calmly, as if he could hardly believe it himself.

'Someone brought me.'

'You were told to come alone.'

I tapped my leg with my cane. 'I'm not driving.'

'You should have taken a cab.'

'And be stuck in Bickley without a ride back to town? No chance.'

'You could have let it wait,' he said.

'It always makes me nervous with a cab outside,' I said. 'The meter ticking away and all. The expense. I don't like it. And if you really thought I was going to walk in here all on my lonesome, you must want your head looking at.'

He ignored the insult. 'So who did drive you?'

'A friend, and my girlfriend came too, just for the ride.'

'You bought a skirt with you,' interrupted Rick.

'Why? You frightened?'

'Of a tart? You're joking.'

'Your mates learnt the hard way.'

'No mates of mine, Sunshine. Don't you fucking listen? Mister Lupino told you.'

'I don't always believe what I hear.'

'You calling my guv'nor a fucking liar?'

Now that was a tough one. I didn't say yes, I didn't say no.

Bim interrupted. 'Where are they?'

'The Lounge Bar,' I said.

'Go and get them,' said Lupino to Rick and Lonzo.

'Watch out, they bite,' I said. 'Especially the black one.'

'You brought a fucking spook with you?' spat Bim.

'Like I said, he brought me.'

'One of Watkins's little firm?'

'Of course.'

'Bring them in,' said Lupino. 'Go on.' Rick and

Lonzo split, picking up two other gangsters as they went like lint on a dark jacket. The band played *The Twist*, which segued into *Let's Twist Again*, followed by *The Peppermint Twist*, and finally *Twistin' The Night Away*. The girls and boys were letting it all hang out. It occurred to me that Chubby Checker had a lot to answer for. Then they moved on to *The Lambada*.

The band worked through its repertoire and I worked through the Smirnoff bottle, never touching the sides once.

After about fifteen minutes Teddy and Fiona were wheeled in by four Greeks. Teddy looked immaculate in his dark suit and Fiona had discarded her coat and was wearing a sexy little black dress that did nothing much to hide her spectacular figure. Everyone in the room clocked the six of them as they entered. Antonia gave Fiona that especially poisonous look that seemed to run in her family. They all came over to our corner of the bar.

'We got the coon and the scrubber,' said Rick proudly.

I made a move towards him but Lupino caught my arm. 'Rick, apologise,' he said. 'You've insulted Mr Sharman's friends.'

Rick looked stunned. 'Do what?'

'You heard,' I said.

'Come, Rick,' said Lupino, suddenly sweet as honey.

'Sorry, Boss,' said Rick. 'I don't know what come over me.'

'Please accept the apology, all of you,' said Bim. 'My boys can be uncouth sometimes.'

'He calls me a scrubber again and I'll kick him in his uncouth bollocks,' said Fiona.

Rick looked stunned again and Lupino showed all his teeth in a long laugh. 'Well said. Come and join us.'

Teddy walked up the steps and beamed me a shit-eating grin. 'Hey, what's happening, man? These guys invited us in and I just couldn't say no.'

'You coons are all heart.'

'And us scrubbers,' said Fiona who had followed him.

'They just couldn't bear to see you all dressed up an' nowhere to go.'

'Nice folks,' said Teddy.

'You OK?' I asked.

'Sure. We'll do.'

His eye caught Antonia who had perked up mightily since he had entered the room. 'Fuck me, who's the Pit Bull?' he asked.

'Boss's daughter. Big cheese.'

'Big fucking doggy. You mean.'

'Check. But it looks like she sure digs you, baby.'

'I told you, man, I'm magic.'

'Don't let the big Bim catch you casting any spells. You know how he feels about the Brothers.'

'Man, give me some credit. I wouldn't touch that old slosher with a barge pole. I got class.'

'And you've got something she likes hidden in your trousers.'

'What, man, my hanky?'

The daughter *was* taking a great interest in Teddy. She spun round on her stool and checked him out. Bim's face suffused with blood. I saw only trouble.

The band changed tempo and got stuck into *Stand By Me* like dogs at a bitch. 'Groovy,' said Teddy. 'Who's the group?'

'James Brown and The Famous Fucking Flames. Live at the Apollo.'

'Burnin',' said Teddy, then raised his voice. 'Hey, can I get a drink?'

'Have some of this.' Antonia got into the action. She lurched off her stool, almost losing her balance as she landed on spiked heels. She advanced up the steps towards us like Godzilla, one hand on the wall to keep her upright and the other holding her half full glass towards Teddy.

'Antonia,' hissed Bim.

'Don't mind if I do,' said Teddy, and took the profferred glass and licked the rim where Antonia's lip print was visible in bright red lip gloss. She looked like she ready to have an orgasm on the spot.

Not a good idea, Teddy, I thought.

'You black bastard!' said Bimpson.

Teddy was too busy gazing over the glass into Antonia's eyes. She was too busy gazing back.

Then I felt a light bulb go on over my head. Now I knew one reason why Bim hated blacks so much. Antonia, his pure, unsullied, unmarried daughter, had hot pants for them. Maybe all his daughters had. Elementary, my dear Sharman.

'Want to dance?' she asked.

Just as she spoke *Stand By Me* groaned to a halt and the band took a moment's break and dived into their glasses. In the dead air before they got going again, I felt all sorts of tensions rising to the surface.

'Get away from her,' said Bimpson. His look was as cold as a frog's backside.

'And if I don't?' asked Teddy.

'You're looking at a world of pain.'

'Hip,' said Teddy. 'Hip, I like that. Listen, man, no way, right? Not with mine, not with yours. Too ugly, man.'

My heart sank. I could not believe I was hearing this.

'But you call me a coon or a black bastard again, and I might take her up on her offer.'

I thought Bimpson Lupino was about to expire of cardiac arrest. So did Rick, who couldn't bear to hear all these insults aimed at his boss's offspring and hauled off and dragged a cracker-jack little .22 out of his back pocket and stuck it in the direction of Teddy's best wool worsted jacket.

I saw the hammer going back so I brought my stick up in a short arc and knocked the barrel away. The sound of the shot was deafening in the confined space, even though it was such a small calibre weapon. It even reached across the room and brought a bossa nova treatment of *A Rainy Night In Georgia* to an early and cacophonous conclusion.

The bullet chopped slivers of wood and sawdust from the top of the bar fitting and screamed off to lodge somewhere in the ceiling. The bar annexe was full of smoke and stank of used gunpowder and cordite. Powder burns spattered Rick's hand and shirt cuff. Teddy looked as if he was in the market for fresh laundry and Rick didn't know whether to be glad he hadn't committed murder or angry that I had stopped him. I stepped back and made a placating gesture. There were still live rounds in the .22's cylinder. Bim grabbed the gun and slammed it down on the bar. I flinched. Accidents do happen. I hoped he hadn't burnt his little mitten on the hot metal. He was in a bad enough mood as it was. Every head in the place turned except Antonia's, whose eyes were glued to Teddy's crotch.

'Later,' Bim said to Rick. The guy actually flinched as if he had been slapped.

Bim got busy appeasing the management. Guests kept peering over, but discreetly. They knew the score. A little gun play at a function was probably nothing new to them. Bim was handing out cash and exchanging favours at a furious rate. I heard him tell the maître d' it was just boyish hi-jinks, all down to the advent of the holiday and too much Christmas spirit.

When he'd finished all the glad handing, Bim came back and grabbed my arm and dragged me over to a private corner. 'That's twice you've got in my face today.'

I just looked at him and said nothing.

'How many times do I have to tell you that I had nothing to do with getting Watkins put away?' Just the way he said it got to me. He seemed old and tired and I almost felt sorry for him.

'All right,' I said. 'I heard.'

'Now get that cheeky fucking spade out of here before I have the black cunt's hands chopped off.' Then I didn't feel sorry for him at all.

I nodded.

'And tell Watkins I'm sorry for his trouble. I'll miss butting heads with him. We've been doing it for over thirty years.'

'I'll do that.'

'Now scarper, and stay away from me and mine.'

I went, collecting Teddy and Fiona.

When we got outside we found that it had been snowing heavily for a long time. It was nearly two inches deep in the car park and we had to clear the windscreen of the jeep before we could leave.

15

Teddy engaged four-wheel drive and the jeep crunched through the snow as sure-footed as a cat. As we headed back to town the snow got thicker. Like I said, he was a good driver, anticipatory and making allowances for the conditions and all the bad drivers the weather had brought out. We saw lots, skating through red traffic lights broadside or spinning their drive wheels uselessly in drifts of snow. He didn't speed, but he seemed to have the knack of picking the right lanes and knowing when to nip through on the inside without bringing out the worst in the other road users. The jeep ploughed through virgin snow and gripped the road like a leech. Teddy played Charlie Parker on the stereo all the way. Not too soft but not too loud because we needed to talk. Sacrilege, but I'm sure old Charlie would have understood.

'What do you think?' asked Teddy, once we were clear of Bickley and all the road signs read 'Central London'.

'He told me he had nothing to do with getting Em put away.'

'He would, wouldn't he? Did you believe him?'

'Funnily enough, yes. Although I think he might know something.'

'Where does that leave us?'

I thought of the five grand burning a hole in my favourite pair of Argyles. 'I don't know. I need time to think.'

'How long?'

'Good question.' I turned around to where Fiona was sitting, curled up in the back in her coat and hat. 'Have you got somewhere to stay?'

'With you,' she said, and her voice told me she felt betrayed by my words.

I shook my head, though I doubted she could see in the darkness. 'No, somewhere safe. Not your place either. I don't want to be worrying about you all the time.'

I thought she was going to argue, but she didn't. Two guns in two days can do that to you. 'There's my dad's,' she said.

'In Waterloo?'

'Yes.'

'Can you go there now?'

'I need a change of clothes.'

'Teddy'll drop us off at your place,' I said. 'OK Teddy?'

'Sure. Do you want me to wait?'

'No.' I replied. 'There's a cab firm local that's quite good, I'll get one to run me home later.'

'I hope you can get one in this weather,' he said.

By this time we were coming to the bottom of the Old Kent Road and the snow was starting to thin out although it still hemmed us in to the cosy interior of the jeep as if we were the last people on earth.

By the time we got to Kennington it had turned colder, the snow had stopped, the sky had cleared and stars shone like sparks of fire splattered across a black curtain. The streets were deserted and the snow was thick on the ground before the morning came and the traffic and pedestrians turned it to foul black slush. But just at that frozen moment the world was as white as to be almost blue under the street lamps. Fiona and I got out of the jeep.

'Are you sure you don't want me to wait?' asked Teddy.

'Sure,' I said. 'You get off home. Call me tomorrow morning.'

'Will do. Take good care of yourself and Fiona.'

'I will.'

'Goodnight Teddy and thanks,' said Fiona.

Fiona and I walked through fresh snow to the entrance of her block. We went up in the lift to the top floor and she let us in to her flat.

'Why can't we stay here?' she asked. 'At least till morning.'

'I don't like it,' I said. 'Just do as I say please. Get some clothes packed and I'll call a cab. Are you going to speak to your dad?'

'Sure,' she said and did so. He answered after a minute. She told him she was coming over and he didn't seem to have any objections.

She went upstairs and I telephoned the local cab service. I'd expected at least an hour's wait but the controller told me five minutes and took the number, and said he'd phone when the cab was outside. Fiona came downstairs with a bag and just as she was about to start complaining again the telephone rang. I answered.

'Cab's downstairs,' said the controller's voice.

'Fine.' I hung up. 'Let's go,' I said to Fiona and we left the flat and took the long lift ride down. On the street outside was parked a dark coloured Cortina estate which flashed its lights as we left the block. We both got into the back of the car.

'Waterloo, then Tulse Hill,' I said.

'Bit iffy on the Tulse Hill bit mate,' said the driver. 'Have you seen the weather?'

'Main roads will be all right,' I said with a confidence I didn't feel. 'We'll do it.'

The cab took off towards the river and when we got to Waterloo Station, Fiona directed the cabby to a small backstreet opposite St Thomas's hospital. He stopped the car and switched off the ignition. I wound down the window for some fresh air. With the engine off the only sound was the rush of the water from the river. Fiona's dad's pre-fab stood in the shadow of the hospital. There were five of the little oblong constructions in a row, each with a tiny patch of garden back and front.

'Give me a ring tomorrow,' I said as she got out. I would have kissed her but I could tell she wasn't keen so I just let her go.

I watched as she walked through virgin snow up the front path of the middle pre-fab and let herself in with a key. She didn't look back. I felt like a bastard, but I've felt that way before and I dare say I will again.

'Tulse Hill,' I said, and the driver started the engine and headed south.

The snow on the ground got thicker but it wasn't too bad on the main roads where previous traffic had cleared the way, and we got to Tulse Hill in about twenty minutes. My street was thick with unmarked snow and the Ford slid and skidded up the slight incline until I pointed out my building made almost unrecognisable by its white cover. I paid the cabby, added a hefty tip and got out. I was yawning by the time I got inside. The flat was warm and silent. I made tea and went to bed but couldn't sleep. Big deal, that had happened before too. I think I dozed towards dawn and when I came to at nine the weather had warmed up considerably and the snow was almost gone, although the man on the radio said it would be back and worse within twenty-four hours. The speed was still dancing in my veins and I couldn't eat so I decided to go and get my car. I was going out on my own later and I needed to be mobile.

Charlie had collected my two cars when it was obvious I was going to be in hospital for a long spell and I didn't want them nicked or vandalised outside my flat. I dawdled around the place for a while, no one called. I phoned for a cab and the driver dropped me at Charlie's just before noon. The streets were filthy by then, just as I'd known they'd be, and I hoped it wouldn't freeze when it got dark.

16

When I got there someone had cleared all the snow off the cars for sale, and polished them. They gleamed in the grey light. Charlie was on the forecourt. He was geeing up a punter as I got out of the cab. The punter was in denims. Charlie had on his working gear: a three-quarter length sheepskin over a double-breasted grey suit, striped shirt and striped tie. Charlie was a serious contender for the oldest yuppie in town. If yuppies still existed.

He didn't see me coming.

The punter was speaking. 'But I can't bring it in,' he said. 'It's broken down in Stepney Green.'

'What can I do, sir?' asked Charlie, as if he didn't know. 'I'm all on my own here apart from an apprentice. Aren't you in the AA?'

'I was about to join but I hardly had time before the car went on the blink. I thought there was a guarantee.'

'Our name is our guarantee,' said Charlie, getting on his high horse. 'Now if you get the car here, I'll get it looked over.'

The punter was going to argue but looking at Charlie's chunky body changed his mind, mumbled something unintelligible and sloped off.

'Looks like he'd rather have the guarantee,' I said.

'Oh, it's you,' said Charlie as if it had been only hours rather than weeks since we'd last spoken. 'If he can't afford to run a decent car he should fuck off.'

'I see that the old "customer's always right" motto still applies,' I said.

'Of course.'

'So has this customer still got any cars here?'

'Naturally.'

'I'm amazed. Are they in running order?'

High horse time again. 'What do you reckon? They're running sweet as nuts.'

'I'm impressed.'

'You've got a fan, or at least the cars have.'

'Who?'

'New mechanic, YTS.'

'Slave labour, you mean.'

'Now, now, Nick. I'm surprised at you. We're living in a venture society, you know.'

'Vulture, more like.'

He opened his arms in surrender.

'What about the motors?' I asked. 'Have you been letting some spotty little git fuck around with them?'

'I told you, they're both running great.'

'With a YTS yobbo screwing them up?'

'The mechanic turns the engines over every other day. Spends too much time with them, if you ask me.'

'Who pays for the gas?'

'The mechanic.'

'Let's see him. I don't usually like mechanics.'

'Oh, you'll like this one.'

'I bet.'

'Tallhulah!' he shouted.

'What?' I said.

A slim figure came out of the workshop. Blonde hair pulled high and tight. Figure like a rake cinched into baggy overalls. You didn't see the bumps until she got close. Not bad bumps at that.

'Tallhulah,' I said.

'Tallhulah,' repeated Charlie.

'Tallhulah,' the girl said. 'That's me. Who wants to know?'

'Tallhulah,' said Charlie, 'this is Nick Sharman.' She could have looked less impressed, but I don't know how.

'I hear you've been taking care of my cars,' I said. 'The "E" and the TransAm?'

'Yes.'

'I've been keeping an eye on them.'

'You must have spent some of your own money on petrol.'

'A bit. It doesn't matter.'

I took out a twenty. 'I'm obliged.'

'I don't want that.'

'Take it, please. I know what you're paid.' And I gave Charlie a dirty look.

'I've got independent means.'

'I bet.'

She hesitated. I didn't do anything dumb like push it into her top pocket. She would have done me for assault.

Eventually she plucked the note from between my fingers. 'The Tranny needs some oil,' she said.

'Just as well I'm taking the E-type then.'

'You'll ruin the bodywork in this mess,' she said, gesturing at the wet pavement. 'The council has salted the roads.'

'Can't be helped. I need a car.'

She looked at me sadly and shook her head. 'Please yourself.'

'Thanks again,' I said to her retreating back.

The cars were tarped up in an extension to the garage proper. The tyres on the E-type were hard and the cellulose shone. There were no visible leaks, and the inside of the cockpit was neat and tidy. The steering wheel was clean and the ignition keys were in the lock. I turned them. The car caught first time, even in the damp air, and soon settled down to a contented purr. I'd have to thank Tallhulah again.

I pulled the car round to the front. Charlie was walking up and down in front of his stock. I noticed that there were more BMWs and Audis and Mercedes than there used to be. Now I understood the threads.

'All right?' he asked.

'Good as gold. Better. If there's anything to pay, stick it on my bill.'

'Your bill, sure. Would you like to see your bill? Because it scares me.'

'Later.'

'Always later, isn't it, Nick? You're lucky I didn't sell one of those heaps to pay it off.'

I winked. 'Cheers, Charlie,' I said and pulled away into the traffic.

17

The car was in great shape. The automatic box was as smooth as twenty-year-old Irish whiskey and the kickdown pushed me back into the leather bucket seat like a giant hand. The car had been suffering a little steering shimmy at about ninety and I'd have to ask Tallhulah to put it on a fast roller for me. The fat tyres splashed through the icy puddles and I had to keep the revs down so as not to lose the rear end on the bends. I tucked my bad leg out of the way and really enjoyed driving again.

I went home and the phone was ringing off the hook. It was Teddy.

'How are you this morning?' he asked.

'Not bad considering. I need to see Em.'

'When?'

'Today.'

'Impossible man. You can't just turn up on the doorstep.'

'Are you seeing him?'

'Sure. Later.'

'Right. I want you to take a message.'

'Like what?'

'Tell him about someone trying to kill me on Thursday night. Tell him about our trip to Bickley.

Tell him I think Bim's straight. And ask him about this Jack Dark geezer who wants to see me.'

'What about him?'

'I want to know if Emerald knows him.'

'OK, man.'

'What time you seeing him?'

'About four.'

'Call me here at seven. I'm off out later.'

'Sure.'

'Make sure you do, Teddy.'

'Sure, man, sure. Relax.'

'It's difficult with so many people shooting guns round me.'

'Sure, man. Later yeah?'

'Later, Teddy,' I said and hung up.

I put the phone down and it rang straight away. I picked up the receiver.

'Nick?' It was Fiona.

'Hi. How are you?' I said.

'Pissed off with you dumping me off like bagwash.'

'Sorry, babe,' I said. 'I was scared for you.'

'Don't be. When can I see you?'

'Soon.'

'When soon?'

'As soon as I've had time to think.'

'About?'

'Everything.'

'Don't go all Sherlock Holmes on me.'

'Never. I've just got a few things to sort out, a few people to see. And I'll feel better if you're safe with your dad.'

'The little woman huh?'

'Don't take it personally. I'll be in touch soon.'

'There's that word again. Just make sure you do.'

'Promise.'

'Promises, Sharman. I've heard them all.'

'This one's a guarantee.'

'I'll take your word for it.'

'I'll see you then,' I said. 'Bye.'

'Bye.'

We hung up.

I killed the afternoon in a bar. I chatted to one of the barmaids who I fancied like mad, but being as she was young enough to be my daughter I kept it light, strictly professional, and tried not to look too hard at her thighs when her micro skirt rode up every time she bent down to get a bottle off the cold shelf.

I stayed late and bought her a drink when her shift finished. I found myself getting less professional and more like a dirty old man as the evening progressed and dragged myself away just before seven to go home. It was cold but not freezing and the weather man said the temperature would drop and the snow come sometime after midnight.

I changed into a dark shirt and black jeans and put on my leather jacket. I slid the envelope full of money into one of the pockets and snapped the fastener.

At seven precisely the telephone rang. It was Teddy.

'Did you see him?' I asked.

'Sure. He sends his regards. Says it sounds like you've been having a wild time.'

'You can say that again.'

'Says he doesn't know about Bim. Says he doesn't know who'd want you dead if it *wasn't* him.

Says he's never heard of Jack Dark. Says watch your arse.'

'Constantly. How is he?'

'Pissed off. Wants to see you. Get you a visiting order soon.'

'I can't wait. An afternoon in Brixton sounds just my style.'

'He says you've been there before.'

'You shouldn't believe everything your uncle says. Look, I've got to go. I'll catch you later.'

We exchanged goodbyes.

I got to the Gray's Inn Road by nine, found the restaurant and parked my car in a side road just opposite. I walked by and peered through the picture window whilst I pretended to study the menu. The place was empty. Two waiters were leaning on the bar inside looking hopeful; one was picking his nose. I hoped I got served by the other.

I went around the side of the block and found a narrow alley that cut through to a small courtyard shadowed by air conditioner vents and smoke extractors and almost full of giant garbage cans on rubber-tyred wheels. It was dark, wet, cold and dismal round there, and water dropped from the eaves of the building and puddled in dank pools on the greasy concrete. The back door to the restaurant was open. I saw two chefs playing pontoon, using a cutting board as a card table.

I went back to the car and moved it a few spaces so that I could watch the front door of the restaurant and the entrance to the alley. I slipped a Steve Earle cassette into the player with the volume low and settled down to wait. I felt that so far that night I would be marked ten out of ten in a private eye exam, only losing points for not having the barmaid waiting for me all warm and willing in bed when I got home. Still, no one's perfect.

As the hands of the clock on the dash crept past nine-thirty a few couples and one party of four young women went into the Mogul Empire. I assumed that Jack Dark wouldn't be alone, and unless he and his cronies dressed in drag it was a no show so far. At nine-forty a big BMW saloon with lights on full beam slid to a halt at the kerb right outside the restaurant. Two guys got out of the front and checked the street. The driver was big, with thick legs in trousers that were so tight they creased like sausage skins around the crotch and knees, but the front seat passenger made the driver look small and when I caught a glimpse of his face I could tell he was a far from happy man. I slid down in my seat and cut the volume on the stereo. When they were both satisfied that the coast was clear, the front passenger walked around the car and opened the rear door on the kerb side and a small man in a long overcoat climbed out and walked across the pavement, closely followed by the huge man who kept his right hand close to the front of his jacket which was open despite the weather.

The driver of the BMW then re-entered the car and drove off. A few minutes later he returned and went into the restaurant after the other two. I swapped Steve Earle for Soloman Burke and waited until ten. At one minute to, I switched off the ignition, climbed out of the car, locked it up and walked across the street. I pushed through the door into the warm spicy smell of the restaurant and the sound of muted sitar music. The three men were not at any of the tables. I stopped and frowned and the waiter who hadn't been picking his nose came over at the double. He was dressed like a snooker player, with a crisp white napkin draped over his arm.

'Sir?' he said. 'You want a table for one?'

I shook my head. 'Mister Dark,' I said. 'He's expecting me.'

'Yes, sir, this way.' And he led me through a door at the back of the restaurant into another room, smaller and with no music playing. At the end of the room was a banquette table with a red leather bench seat in the shape of a squared off 'U' which would have comfortably seated eight people. The small man who had been in the back of the BMW was sitting on the far side of the table facing the door, and the huge man was sitting on his left where that side of the bench jutted out into the room, taking up enough room for two. The table was covered with dishes of food and the pair had half-empty plates and beer glasses in front of them. The driver was sitting on an upright chair just inside the door. His thick legs blocked the entrance.

'Excuse me,' I said.

'Sharman?' asked the driver. He wasn't my mystery caller. His voice was lighter and the accent came from up north somewhere.

' 'S'right,' I said.

'You don't look like much,' he said. Liverpool, I might have guessed. I've never been keen on people from Liverpool.

'Cheers,' I said back, and the driver moved his

legs. I walked to the table where the two men sat.
They both stopped eating and looked at me. 'Mister
Dark?' I said with a query in my voice, and the
smaller of the two men nodded. The other man
stopped me with a raised hand, slid out of his seat
and stood. Christ, but he was big close up.

'Lift your arms,' he said. He was my telephone
chum all right, hoarse and Cockney. I did as I was
told and he searched me. His jacket was still unbut-
toned and there was a bulge under his left armpit.
Mind you, this cat bulged all over, but this particular bulge was not of flesh and blood. The smaller,
older man chewed and stared at me as I was being
frisked. The huge man found my cigarettes, lighter,
car keys and the bag of money, all of which he carefully placed on an empty table next to theirs. When
he was finished, he said, 'He's clean.'

'In mind and body,' I said. The huge man snarled
and said nothing.

'You're punctual,' said the smaller man. 'I like
that. Sit down.' He pointed at the seat directly to his
left.

I remained standing. 'I'm not sure that I'm staying
yet,' I said. 'I just came to give you your money back.'

'I don't want it back,' said the small man. 'Like
you were told on the phone, it's a gesture of good
faith.'

'People I don't know are rarely that good to me, or
that faithful,' I said. Christ, people I do know aren't.

'I just want to talk,' he said. 'No big deal. After all,
it's a long way to come for nothing.' He paused.
'What have you got to lose?'

I shrugged.

'Sit down then,' he said, and after twenty seconds

or so I concurred. The huge man stood aside. I tossed my stick in ahead of me and slid down the slippery seat. He sat down on my left, effectively blocking my way out. It was all done in a friendly and casual way but it immediately put me at a disadvantage, or so they thought.

'Something to eat?' asked the small man.

'No thanks.'

'Go on, the food's fucking brilliant here. Try this.' He picked up a clean fork and handed it to me, indicating a dish that was keeping hot on one of those funny little heaters with the nightlights inside that they always put on the tables at Indian restaurants, and you always touch because you can't believe it will be hot enough to keep food bubbling, and you always burn your hand. I accepted the fork and took a little of the meat and sauce and tasted it. It was like sticking my mouth on to the damn heater. Tears filled my eyes.

'Jesus!' I said.

The little man grinned and showed a mouthful of gold. 'Special mutton vindaloo,' he said. 'They make it for me every Saturday night. I do love a hot curry. I spent time out in India in the sixties.' He put his hand over the table, palm down, and wiggled it about like people like him do when they're trying to show you how smart they are. 'A bit of dodgy import and export.' He winked. 'Know what I mean?'

I did but said nothing. I was too busy dabbing at my eyes with a napkin.

'I got the taste out there,' he went on, and grinned again like he was the cleverest little fucker in town.

I drank some iced water and felt better.

'You look like you could use a beer,' the small man said.

'Kingfisher, cold.'

'Jim, get him what he wants,' the small man said and the driver got up obediently and vanished through the door into the main restaurant.

The driver came back with two bottles of freezing beer and a glass.

'Jim,' the small man introduced the driver as he put the bottles and glass on the table. 'And next to you is Ronnie. He's my boy, looks after me.'

I didn't think I was supposed to shake hands, so I just looked at the men who imperceptibly nodded. Jim went back to his place by the door.

'What can I do for you?' I asked.

'Have something to eat,' said Jack Dark. I could see we were going to go at his speed and I gave in.

'Not that,' I said, indicating the dish in front of him.

'Have what you like,' he said. 'Jim, get the waiter.'

He jumped up again and stuck his head out into the main restaurant and said something I couldn't hear. A moment later the waiter who had greeted me scooted in and stood to attention beside our table. 'Feed this man,' said Jack Dark.

'Sir?' said the waiter.

'I'll have tandoori king prawn,' I said. 'Aloo gobi, Niramish, cauliflower bhajee and some pilau rice, and a sweet nan with raitha.'

Jack Dark wrinkled his nose. 'Baby food,' he said to me, then to the waiter, 'bring me and Ronnie another round of vindaloo with boiled rice and lime pickle and some more chillis in vinegar, and see what Jim wants, and get us four more beers.'

The waiter nodded and finished writing down the order. On his way out he stopped by Jim who shook his head and said something about Paki muck. The waiter shrugged and left and shut the door behind him.

'Jim likes steak and chips,' said Jack Dark by way of explanation.

I couldn't have cared less if Jim liked to chew on the maroon flock wallpaper that hung in the restaurant, with ketchup. 'Do you always get a private room?' I asked.

'Sure, they do well out of me here,' said Jack Dark.

'In used notes,' I said, and he showed me his gold teeth again. 'You wanted to talk,' I said. 'So let's talk.'

'Right,' said Jack Dark. He drank some beer, sat back and belched. 'Ronnie here tells me you don't know me.'

I nodded in agreement, but didn't say I wasn't sure I wanted to, although I wasn't.

'You know what I do, though,' he said confidently.

'Do I?' I asked, puzzled.

'Sure you do. If you live in London, you know what I do.'

'Give me a clue.'

'Walk down any main street and you'll see my handiwork.'

'You train dogs to shit on the pavement,' I said.

He looked angry for a second, then he laughed. 'Train dogs to shit on the pavement,' he said. 'I like that. Did you hear that, Jim? Ronnie? Train dogs to shit on the pavement. I'll have to remember that.'

Ronnie didn't look any too amused but I gave him a big grin anyway. 'So that's not it?'

'No,' said Jack Dark.

I was patient. The smell of food was making me hungry, the beer was strong, and I reckoned I was good for an hour before I got bored and left. 'So tell me.'

He said the name of a well-known high street jeweller. One that seemed to have a branch in every area and every shopping precinct in the south. Cheap and nasty. 'Shit in boxes,' as an old mate of mine who ran a market stall would say.

'That's me,' he said proudly.

'I'm not surprised,' I said.

'Meaning?'

I shrugged. 'Nothing,' I said. 'But what's it got to do with me?'

'I'm losing stock. I need someone to check on the losses and your name came up.'

'Where from?'

'Just around and about, you know.'

'No, I don't.'

'Of course you do.'

'Is that right?'

'That's dead right. Are you interested?'

'A store detective?'

'Sort of, but I'm convinced it's the staff that's getting away with ninety per cent of the gear, maybe more.'

'A spy then?'

'Yeah.'

'I don't really think that that's my style. You need

more than one operative for a job like that. A big company would suit you better. You'd need to plant people in the shops where the losses were greatest. Anyone who was nicking would suss me out in a minute. Your losses might stop in that outlet, but as soon as I left they'd start again. I imagine most of the people who work for you are young.'

He nodded.

'That's what I mean, your people would never trust me. You'd need young kids to go in, no one would suspect them. And you could move them around from branch to branch to make it look better. But it still might take months to get a result. Take my advice, have your cash back and use it better elsewhere.'

'You're turning down five grand?'

'Yeah, I don't want to rip you off.'

'You wouldn't. Look, do me a favour. Come in as my security officer. You don't have to do the donkey work yourself. If you need kids, hire kids. I don't care what it costs.'

'You've got security,' I said. 'Plenty of it. And if you're chucking five grand around, you can get plenty more. I still say a big firm would do you better.'

'Perhaps there are things that you can do that a big firm can't or won't.' He made as if to say something more, but I interrupted.

'Wait just a minute,' I said, 'before we go any further. I don't carry a gun anymore, and I'm not popular with the law. So if you think you've got a likely lad who'll do a serious naughty for that sort of dough, you'd better think again.'

'I know that,' he said. 'I need exactly what I said

I needed, a security consultant, kosher. I want you to find out what's going on and tell me, and I'll take care of the rest.'

'What rest?'

'You don't need to know about that.'

'On the contrary, Mr Dark, I need to know exactly that. I don't kill people and I don't finger people to be killed. Especially for a few gold-plated chains. I've got a very delicate conscience these days and I like to sleep nights.'

That *was* a joke.

'You're not like I thought you'd be,' he said.

'Who is?' I asked, and laughed, and so did he. The atmosphere eased and somewhere in the back of the building a bell rang. A couple of minutes later the waiter came in wheeling a trolley stacked high with food. We were silent whilst he cleared the empty dishes from our table and filled it up again, explaining what was in each dish as he put it out. He gave us clean, hot plates, fresh cutlery and more beers, and then split. We all loaded our plates and started to eat.

18

As I chased a king prawn, charcoaled almost black in the tandoori oven, around my plate with a fork, I took the opportunity to study Jack Dark a little closer.

He had a face like a weasel on heat with cheeks and chin shaved as smooth as the inside of a tin can even at that late hour of the day. He was wearing a black, roll-neck sweater under a blue double-breasted blazer with fine hand stitching on the lapels and gold buttons that gleamed like minia-ture suns under the spotlights in the restaurant. With it he wore houndstooth check grey trousers that he'd probably picked up in a little boutique in Romford or Ilford with just one subtlely lit Hugo Boss suit in the window and an assistant who doesn't tell you the price tag until you've had the alterations done. And, man, if you had to ask, you shouldn't have been trying it on in the first place.

With the combo he wore plenty of male jewellery. A gold chain around the outside of the roll neck supported a large gold medallion with what I thought was a likeness of Napoleon on the outside. On his left pinky he wore a gold signet ring. On his wedding finger he wore a thick, plain gold band. On his third finger right hand he wore a gold sovereign ring, and on that pinky, a thin gold ring set with rubies. On his left wrist was a genuine, gold Rolex Oyster with chips of diamonds set around the bevel and more chips of diamond for the numerals, so that the whole thing reflected the lights like a mirror. It was a little overstated for Gray's Inn Road, I thought, but all right for Stringfellow's after midnight to order drinks heliographically. I would have taken bets that skinny-arsed women in Spandex tights wet their G-strings over that particular male fashion accessory.

Although I couldn't see them I would have put my winnings on the fact that he wore Gucci loafers with discreet gold chains. All in all, the boy was a walking gold mine. It was just as well he owned a string of jewellers.

There was only one problem that I could see. With all the glitter and the Italian clobber that cost a bomb, on top of his head was perched an Irish that wouldn't have fooled a blind man in a heavy thunderstorm. I suppose he thought it made him look young or sexy, or both. It didn't. It made him look old and foolish. It was sort of bright ginger that didn't go with the grey hair that grew at the back and sides of his head. The heat of the food he was chucking down his neck was making him sweat, and the sweat had sort of floated the wig out of whack. I thought that one of his boys would have sent him a late news flash about that particular item. No points out of ten for that, Jack, I thought.

As we ate, he chatted away like we were old friends. He told me about his wife and daughters, but I really didn't listen. When his plate was empty and carefully wiped with a piece of nan bread, he looked up. 'Well?' he said. 'What do you say? Do you want the job?'

'No, Jack,' I said back. 'It's a nice offer but I think I'll pass. I've got other things to do and I wouldn't be able to give you the sort of attention you need. No hard feelings, I hope?' It occurred to me that at this point in my life I was making enough enemies without adding Jack Dark and his little firm.

'I'm not used to people saying no to me.'

'I'm sure.'

He thought for a minute. 'I'll tell you what,' he said. 'Take the cash anyway, forget the job. Go on holiday. You can have a good couple of weeks with five K. Go to the West Indies. We had a cracking holiday in St Lucia last Christmas. Warm? Christ, I'll say it was! You'll love it. Take a sort with you. I'm sure you've got one or two tucked away, a good-looking boy like you. It'll do wonders for your bad leg, the sun and that. You'll be able to throw that stick away when you get home.'

'Swimming,' piped up Jim from his seat by the door, where he'd obviously been listening to every word. 'Good for bad legs, swimming.' And shut up.

'Jim's right,' said Jack. 'Do yourself a favour, take the dough and the holiday. Take Fiona away, she could do with a break. She's been looking a bit peaky lately.'

I didn't like him mentioning Fiona one bit. 'What do you know about her?' I asked. He didn't reply, just sort of smirked which really pissed me off. 'No, Jack,' I said. 'I don't like the feel of this one bit. Bodyguards and dirty money and buckshee holidays in the sun, and you knowing about my girlfriend. It's too strange for me to comprehend. And when things get strange, I get going. Keep your money, I don't want it.'

'You're not going anywhere,' said Ronnie, and all of a sudden I knew why he was armed and we were in a private room. Five grand for my life. Good fucking deal, Jack. But I'd turned the deal down, so I was in trouble. I wondered if they were going to have coffee served before they took me out, and that pissed me off more.

'Who's going to stop me?' I said, and looked over at Jack. 'Neither of these two Herberts, I'll bet. I was watching you tonight when you arrived, Jack. It was all very moody with the big car and the two minders checking the street. But they didn't check me and I could have been sitting in my car with a sniper's rifle and blown your kidneys away before they even realised I was on the same planet.

'Also, it's not a very good idea for it to be known that you have a regular Saturday night nosh up here. Let's face it, anyone and his uncle could pop in for a quick take out chicken birianhi and stick their hand around that door there –' I looked down to where Jim was sitting, listening, and then back to Jack '– and blow your fucking head off before either of these two berks could stop them.'

'Who are you calling a berk?' said Ronnie.

'You,' I said, and pushed the dish with the remains of my raitha on to his lap with my elbow. The yoghurt and cucumber mix splattered the blue serge of his trousers. He jumped up awkwardly in the confined space between the bench seat and the table and pulled back his suit coat to save the material. He spat out a one-syllable word that I didn't hear properly but I'm sure rhymed with 'hunt'. I stood with him. I put my right hand inside his jacket and found the butt of the pistol I knew was there. It slid smoothly out of its talcum-powdered holster. I pulled it free and stuck the barrel in the fleshy part of his neck between ear and jawbone, and hooked back the hammer. It was a big old Smith and Wesson revolver, a real Dirty Harry gun, probably chambered for .357 or .44 magnum ammo, with the front sight smoothed down and the rear sight removed so that it wouldn't snag. It hadn't. There was no safety catch on that beauty and the action engaged with an oily click. The last time I'd stuck a S&W into someone's face, they'd pissed themselves. At least, I think it was the last time. In my exciting world one tends to lose count. I was pretty sure that Ronnie wasn't going to do the same.

I resisted the temptation to make like Clint Eastwood, I didn't need to. Ronnie wasn't stupid. He stayed stock still, one hand holding the skirt of his coat back and the other flat on the table, supporting himself. Jim, however, was a different matter. As soon as he saw what was going off he hit the floor and started crawling towards the cover of the nearest table. His big arse encased in tight grey serge trousers with a VPL that would make your eyes water was a tempting target but I simply said, 'Freeze, you scouse git.' He kept going like a beached whale making for an enticing breaker across a beach of patterned Wilton, and I said, 'Jim, stop or you'll have two arseholes, I swear.' He stopped. 'Lie flat and spread your arms. And, Jack, hands where I can see them please.' He obligingly put his hands palms down on the tablecloth. 'Has Jim got a gun?' I said to Ronnie. 'Tell me the truth or else.'

He nodded.

'Jim,' I said, 'sit up and take the gun out. Slowly now, using just your fingertips.' He did as he was told and pulled out a Beretta 934. He held it like it was hot. 'Take out the clip, and put it on the floor.' He did. 'Now put on the safety and clear and action, and don't touch the trigger.' He did that too, and showed me. There was nothing in the breech. 'Stand up and put the lot on the table.' He obeyed.

I reached over with my left hand and picked up the gun and full clip and pushed them into one of the big pockets in my leather jacket. 'Now sit down somewhere quiet, Jim, not too close, not too far away, and put your hands flat on the table in front of you.'

He pulled out a chair from the next table and sat down. I looked around the quiet room and wondered what to do next. When you've got a gun stuck in someone's face, there's not a lot more you can do. You've got everyone's attention, which presumably was what you wanted in the first place, and that's it. Unless of course you want to get extremely brisk and use the thing. I didn't.

'Right,' I said. 'Everyone stay calm and no one will get hurt. Ronnie, go and sit next to Jim, and wipe your trousers. If that dries you'll never get the stain out.' Much to my surprise, he did. Sit down that is, not wipe his trousers. He must have had more than one suit.

See, that's another problem with guns. In the

movies, if someone pulls out a firearm, everyone does exactly as they're told. In real life, sometimes they just look at you and laugh. I thought I'd better go with the flow, whilst the going was good.

'Jack,' I said, 'I don't even know if you're who you say you are, and I've got a feeling I'm going to want to see you again. Empty your pockets.'

'Make me.'

See what I mean?

'Don't fuck with me, Jack,' I said. 'I'm not in the mood.' And I leant over and stuck the muzzle of the S&W right on to the medallion he was wearing on his chest. 'Are you going to do what I tell you, or what?' He licked his lips and I knew I had him. 'Do it,' I said. He did.

'I'm definitely going to have your bollocks for door stops,' he growled.

I didn't really listen. I would have said the same under the circumstances. I pulled the gun back and he went to reach inside his jacket. 'No, Jack,' I said.

'It's my wallet,' he protested.

'Fine. Just pull the jacket open, both sides, slowly.' He did. No weapon. 'Get it,' I said, and he tugged a wallet from his inside pocket. He pushed it across the table and I flipped it open. Money, plenty, which I left untouched. Credit cards, lots, in clear plastic holders that opened like a concertina. MR JACK P. DARK was embossed on the front of each one. 'Good,' I said. 'At least the name's the same.' I found business cards in a pocket under a flap. On the front was his name, the name of the jeweller's and an address in Hatton Garden. On the back was an address in Emerson Park and an Essex phone code. Emerson Park, I knew it. An

Essex boy if ever I saw one. Fucking Essex, what a dump. It's a pity some transport minister or other hadn't concreted the whole county over years ago, and made it into a parking lot for the rest of us.

I put the card in my pocket and threw the wallet on the table. 'I'm going now, and I don't want anybody to follow me,' I said, and picked up my stick and cigarettes and car keys. I left the envelope full of money on the table and made for the door. I know I should have asked more questions, but it was a tricky situation, three on one, even if I did hold the firepower, and the waiter could have come back at any moment and raised the alarm. So like before, when the going was good, I went.

Ronnie turned his head and studied me closely as I walked across the room. I felt like a specimen on a slide. 'One day, you and me are going to meet again,' he said.

'But until then, Ronnie,' I said, 'be good. And if you can't be good, be careful.'

'You be careful, Sharman. Don't go walking down no dark alleys alone at night.'

'Ronnie, like I told you before, I'm not that kind of girl.'

And on that note I opened the door and split. The pistol I was holding went in my other jacket pocket.

The temperature seemed to be dropping again when I left the restaurant. I limped into a run and got to the car, started it and pulled away as fast as I could. No one else left the restaurant, not by the front door anyway. I played the radio softly as I drove back across London and the weather man told me that within a couple of hours we were due a small blizzard. I looked through the half-open window beside me and saw the stars and shrugged off the idea.

I turned up the volume on the radio when it started playing music again.

I wondered what Jack Dark's game was. It had to be to do with Emerald. But how and why? Emerald didn't know him. Teddy didn't know him. Dark himself hadn't mentioned the case. He just wanted me otherwise engaged. Doing some spurious job, on holiday or dead. Were Jack Dark and Bim connected? I doubted it. I'd believed Bim when he'd told me he had nothing to do with Emerald's trouble, and I still did. He was an elderly man getting older every day. He seemed to be mellowing, if you could call his behaviour mellow. What he must have been like in the old days didn't bear thinking about.

I parked the Jaguar on the forecourt when I got home and let myself in. The telephone was ringing when I opened my flat door. I dropped my keys and grabbed the receiver without putting on the lights.

The moon shone through the open curtains and turned the skin on my hand the colour of a fresh corpse. ' 'Lo,' I said.

'Is that Nick Sharman?' It was a male voice I didn't know, and it occurred to me how many new, fun people I'd met over the past few days.

'That's me.'

'You don't know me, but I need to talk to you.'

'Really?'

'That's right.'

'And you are?'

'My name's Taylor, Lawrence Taylor.' He sounded nervous.

'You're right, Lawrence,' I said. 'I don't know you.'

'But I still need to talk to you, now.'

'About?'

'Not on the telephone.'

'That narrows the options, Lawrence,' I said. 'I'm a bit larey of meeting strangers at night in strange places. Can you come here tomorrow?'

'No, that's impossible. It has to be tonight.'

'Where then?'

'Here.'

'Where's here?'

He gave me an address in Kennington, and told me it was the top flat. 'Wait a minute,' I said. 'I'm in the dark.' I put down the receiver. I drew the curtains and switched on a table lamp and found a pad and pencil and went back to the phone. It was dead. I tried to summon him from the air, but it was no go. I hung up and jotted down the address he'd given me, and went and got a beer from the fridge. I drank it as I smoked a cigarette and paced the floor and wondered if he'd ring back. He didn't. There was something about it I didn't like. I turned off the light and pulled back one curtain and looked into the street. It was a beautiful night. I was all alone and felt like shit. That's life. I toyed with the idea of going out again, but nished it. I told myself I didn't need the aggravation. But really I think I was scared. I felt I was running out of luck. How right I was.

Eventually I undressed and got into bed and took a pill and fell asleep listening to the radio. I hardly even noticed that the other half of my bed was empty.

19

I slept badly and dreamed that I was tangled up in a telephone line that went on forever. I could only get through to strangers who couldn't understand me, and the only people I could understand whispered down the line about my death. I woke up with a start, all caught up in my own damp bedsheets. The first thing I saw, on the bedside table next to the lamp, was the piece of paper with the address in Kennington. I knew that I should have gone there when Lawrence Taylor had phoned the previous night.

I looked at the clock. Seven oh five it read, and something was out of kilter. Even with the curtains drawn the room seemed strangely light. I got up and drew them back. The weather man on the radio had been right. The snow was thick outside and the street was bright from the reflections of the street lamps even though the sky was still dark. My car was just a white hump on more white. The road and pavements were hardly touched by tracks that early on a Sunday morning and I knew I'd never make even the short run up to Kennington in the Jag.

I called Teddy. The telephone rang and rang and I was just about to give up when he answered.

'What?'

'And a very good morning to you too, Teddy.'

'Who's that?'

'Nick.'

'Christ, what time is it?'

'Time you were up and out, my son.'

'What? Where? Why?' He seemed to cover most of the possibilities.

'Have you seen the state of the weather?'

'No, what's the matter with it?'

'Never mind. Is that vanilla slice of yours gassed up?'

He hesitated. 'Yeah.'

'Then get it over here, right away.'

'Why?'

'Take a look out of the window. They do have windows in Peckham, don't they?'

'Yeah.'

'Then look,' I said patiently.

The phone went down with a bang. He was back in a minute, sounding a bit more alive. 'I see what you mean,' he said. 'Where are we going?'

'I'll tell you when I see you. Now get her out and yourself too.'

'Who? There's no one here.'

'A celibate Mister Super Bad. That's a novelty.'

'A fact though, if it's any of your business. Who were you sleeping with last night that was so special?' he asked nastily.

'I give in,' I said. 'Just get here, it's important.' And I put down the telephone.

He arrived just before eight, just as it was getting fully light. I was watching the wind blow powdered snow to fill in the few footsteps and tyre tracks that marred the smooth surface of the street when the

Suzuki pulled up. I went down to meet him. He was standing in the street with snow past his ankles when I got downstairs. He was wearing a jean jacket over a thick sweater and blue jeans tucked into black, calf-length, sheepskin-lined boots. I wore last night's jeans and my Schott with a pair of hightop Doc Martens and black leather gloves. I had pulled a thick, black, woollen watch cap over my hair to keep in the heat. I carried a loaded gun in each jacket pocket.

It was bloody freezing in the street and I wished I had stayed in bed.

I trudged through the snow, carrying my stick. It was pretty well redundant if not downright dangerous in the weather conditions. Teddy stayed by the jeep and watched me coming. When I reached him, I said, 'I don't want to hang around. Let's go.' Gingerly I found the edge of the kerb, kicked through the snow in the gutter and went round to the passenger door of the car. It was warm inside but draughty from the gaps between the fastenings of the soft top. Teddy got in and switched on the engine and hot air blew through the vents under the dash.

'What's all this about? he asked.

I told him. About Jack Dark and the money and our aborted dinner date, and about the telephone call from Lawrence Taylor.

He looked at me oddly when I finished. 'Who's Lawrence Taylor?'

'Who knows?'

'How do you know it's about all this?'

'Because everything lately's about all this,' I replied. 'But if it's because I haven't paid my milk bill and Lawrence Taylor is a special investigator for the United Dairies, I'll apologise for dragging you out in the snow and buy you breakfast, if we can find a café that's open.' I lit a cigarette. 'Are you going to take me?'

He didn't look happy. 'I'll take you.'

'Let's go then. Time's a wasting.'

He put the jeep into gear, pulled out into the middle of the street and pointed it north.

The roads were almost deserted as we went. One or two cars, a few newspaper delivery trucks and a couple of buses trying to maintain some sort of service, but the stops were deserted and pedestrians few and far between. The closer we got to the centre of town, the clearer the main streets got, but not much clearer.

I'd checked in the A–Z before I left the flat and directed Teddy down the Kennington Road, which wasn't too bad for snow, and then right and sharp left into a narrow street of terraced houses where it lay thick and untouched. I squinted through the side window past Teddy's head. 'There,' I said. 'On the left, park down a bit.' He did as I directed and switched off the engine. I could hear the wind whistling against the side of the vehicle. I pulled the two guns from my pockets and held them, one in each hand. Teddy's eyes widened. 'Can you use one of these?' I asked.

He nodded.

'Which one do you want?'

'The revolver,' he said.

I passed the S&W to him, cocked and locked the Beretta and put it back in my jacket. We left the jeep and stepped back into the bitter wind which pasted my jeans to my legs and made me want to piss. I didn't take my stick. Teddy was still holding the magnum. 'Get that out of sight,' I hissed.

He pulled up his jacket and pushed the gun down the front of his jeans, pulling the jacket back over the butt of the pistol. I winced. 'Don't blow your balls off.'

'Don't worry, I won't. Which number do we want?'

'Number 28, top flat,' I said. 'Let's go.' We went up to the door of the house. The carpet of snow over the short path from the pavement was trampled flat. Two bells, both tagged. Top one in the name of Murray, bottom one Johnson. Neither name meant anything to me. I rang the top bell. No answer. I rang it again. Same. I rang the bottom bell. No answer. Again. Same.

'What do we do now?' asked Teddy. 'Kick the door down?'

I ran my hand along the top of the door frame and came away with dirty finger tips to my gloves and a Yale key.

'Yeah,' I said. 'Let's kick the door down. Let's make a nice racket, this early on a Sunday morning. You're good, you know that, Teddy? Someone's been and gone here. I don't like it.'

I put the key in the lock and opened the door. We were in a tiny hall hardly big enough to accommodate the pair of us, facing two half glass doors, one with a brass 'A' screwed to the woodwork, one with a brass 'B'. 'A' was closed tight. 'B' was open six inches or so, just wide enough to see a slice of stairway leading upwards. My stomach did a back flip. I've learned to distrust doors that should be locked standing open and inviting. I took the Beretta out of my pocket, slipped off the safety and held the gun in my left hand. I saw my other arm stretch, almost of its own volition, and the gloved hand push the door wide.

I walked through and felt warm, fetid air. I turned to Teddy. 'I've got a bad feeling about all this,' I said. My chest was pounding and I found it hard to breathe. I wanted to turn and run, just go anywhere that the air was fresh and fear didn't wait behind every open door.

I started up the single flight that seemed to stretch for miles. I heard music softly playing above, and something else, like an electric alarm clock, going off further away.

The central heating had been turned up full. The radiator on the stairs was bubbling and nearly burnt me, even though I only touched it for a second and was wearing gloves.

The music stopped and so did we. I heard the click of an automatic turntable through the silence and the song started again. *Me And Mrs Jones*, it was, by Billy Paul. I can never listen to that song now.

I got to the top of the stairs and Teddy was right behind me. There was a passage leading away to the back of the house, decorated with flowered wallpaper in colours nature never intended. It contained four closed doors, all painted white and fitted with naff silver handles, like council issue. I opened the nearest. Toilet and bathroom combined, all clean and neat and feminine. Opposite was the living room, curtains drawn, one table lamp lit. A Scotch bottle and two dirty glasses on the coffee table. Billy Paul on a cheap stereo. It was so hot I was all wet under my clothes and wiped sweat from the stubble on my chin.

The third room was the bedroom.

I pushed the door open. The curtains were drawn and the central light was on.

Teddy was right behind me.

The room smelled like an open bowel. It was small and seemed crowded with too much furniture. A large wardrobe with sliding doors, a dressing table cluttered with bottles and tubes, a flounced stool, a chest of drawers and a large double bed that had been pulled away from the wall into the middle of the flashily patterned carpet. The bed linen and pillows had been pulled off and scattered across the room. There were clothes twisted and balled in the sheets and duvet. The mattress was covered with a mixture of blood, shit and piss that had set to the consistency of the filling of a lemon meringue pie. It was thick and brown with a black crust around the edges that looked like it would crack if you touched it.

A still figure lay face down, half on and half off the bed. It was a woman. She was naked except for a black bra. The handle of a chisel or a screwdriver protruded from between her legs, poking obscenely upwards. The wood was smeared with blood dried to a rust colour. Her hands and feet were tied with cords and the flesh was black and swollen around the bonds.

Squeamishly I gripped her shoulder and turned her over. She rolled out of the gunk with a sucking sound, expelling foul air from her mouth and sexual organs, and I looked at a face straight out of a nightmare.

Her features had set in a rictus of agony. Someone had cut her lips off and the ragged edges of her
mouth were drawn over yellow gums. Her open
mouth was full of clotted blood. Her throat had
been cut into another mouth and someone had
carved WHORE on the skin of her chest above the
bra.

'Oh, Jesus,' I said. 'What the fuck is going on?' I
heaved and tasted a bile of curry in the back of my
throat. My eyes blurred with tears and I put my
hand on the wall and lowered my head as if to block
out the images of inhumanity and death.

Teddy put his hand to his mouth. 'Don't be sick in
here,' I said. 'Don't you fucking dare! Go to the
bathroom or get out, but don't let anyone see you.'

He went to the bathroom. I left the bedroom after
him and closed the door behind me. I stood in the
hallway, back against the wall, head bowed, trying
to find some fresh air to breathe. I heard Teddy
force the bathroom window open and felt a small,
cold breeze. I gulped at the cool freshness of it. He
came out of the bathroom with a towel over the
lower part of his face. Billy Paul was still singing
about having it off with someone else's wife. I was
getting sick and tired of the tune.

'Turn that fucking racket off, will you?' I saw
Teddy's eyes above the white edge of the towel and
there was something strange in his expression, but
he went into the living room and the music stopped.

I made for the last door.

Big mistake.

The smell in the kitchen was even worse than in
the bedroom, if that was possible. The air was
thick and rancid and the smoke detector was

bleeping. That was the noise I had heard before. Something, *someone*, was lying across the burners of the electric cooker. A white geezer I'd never seen before and didn't want to see again in a hurry. He'd been left on a low heat, naked, simmering. His eyes bulged with milky secretion and his hair had been burnt, so that what remained was glazed on his blistered scalp like charcoal. The skin and flesh that touched the hobs was done to a crisp.

He was as dead as dead could be, and over-cooked.

I heard Teddy come in behind me and turned. I wanted to warn him, but his arm was raised and came down and the pistol in his hand crashed against my head and the room tilted and splintered into a million gilded sparks of blood red and orange and I plunged into darkness like a diver making the longest dive of his life.

20

The sound of an emergency klaxon brought me round with a jump. For a few seconds I didn't know where I was or what was going on. But when I tasted curry again and smelt cooking human flesh, I remembered, and knew it would be a week or two before pork featured in my diet. Then I thought of prison food and the thought brought me to my knees and up to my feet, nearly keeling over as the dizziness and pain hit me. I righted myself by holding on to the kitchen table. There was blood in my eyes, blood on my hands, blood in my mouth and bloody murder on my mind. Teddy and the two guns were gone. Luckily the woollen watch cap I was wearing had taken some of the power out of his blow.

I looked around in panic. I heard voices and footsteps below. There was a door in front of me, key in lock and double bolted. I cracked the bolts, turned the key, opened the door and looked down a steep metal fire escape. I slammed the door behind me, locked it from the outside and threw the key as far away as I could.

The steps of the escape were slick with ice and rust and I blessed old Doctor Marten for the grip his boots gave me. I half jumped, half slid down the steps, kicked aside a pile of black garbage sacks and beat a path to the back gate. It stuck and I felt fingernails break inside my glove as I dragged it open. Outside the gate was a narrow alley, running right to left, and facing me another back gate. I pulled it open and ran through the garden, up a passage at the side of the house and over a set of iron railings into the Kennington Road.

A bus was just pulling up at a stop and the doors opened with an hydraulic sigh. An old dear clambered on board and I clambered after her, exhibiting considerably less agility. I pulled out a tenner and asked for a sixty pence ticket. The driver gave me a dirty look. 'I can't change that,' he said and clocked the state of my boat race. God alone knew what I looked like. I heard sirens in the distance. 'Keep it,' I said.

He heard the sirens too and hesitated, then took the note and worked the switch that closed the doors, engaged gear and pulled away. I fell into the seat reserved for the handicapped and people with shopping or babies and held tightly to the chrome bar, watching the world and the police cars go by. I felt every eye in the bus on me. I closed mine and sank back against the vibrating window.

When I opened my eyes again Kennington had merged into Brixton. I didn't know what bus I was on, where it was headed or how far I could travel, but I figured for a cockle I was all right for a trip to the terminus and a cup of tea in the canteen.

The bus reached Brixton Hill and I passed streets I recognised. Wanda the Cat Woman lived close by and I needed sanctuary. The bus lurched up past the prison where Emerald was probably just finishing his breakfast and, if I wasn't careful, I'd soon be joining him for some porridge of my own. I saw a request stop looming, rang the bell and hit the pavement.

I was starting to crash and crash heavily. My eyes weren't focusing and every small step was a giant leap. I would gratefully have curled up in the gutter and slept until a Lambeth Council mechanical sweeper came and plucked me from my temporary bed.

I headed up Brixton Hill, slipping and sliding on the packed snow, then turned left by a big council estate and found Wanda's house down on the corner. I rubbed some snow over my face to clean it and clear my head. I pushed open the garden gate and walked up the path. I leaned on the bell and felt myself going again. I was being watched by an audience of cats sitting in the front room window. There seemed to be dozens of them and the inside of the glass was cloudy from their breath. They looked disdainfully on as I slumped against the door jamb.

I was beginning to wonder what the hell I was doing there when the door opened and I fell into the passage. I registered blonde hair, a Japanese kimono and a smell of cats, and a voice said 'Hello, Nick, have you been at the glue again?' before sweet darkness enveloped me once more.

21

When I came to, I was in a vast, soft bed. But I woke
with such a start that I imagined I was back in that
dreadful kitchen with a dead body cooking on the
stove. I must have been clutching the sheet and
sweating in panic for two minutes before I realised
I was safe.

I stank and my mouth tasted like the inside of a
soil pipe. I shouted some gobbledegook as I came
up from unconsciousness and Wanda appeared in
the bedroom doorway, looking cool but concerned.

'Good morning, Nicholas.'

'Hi.'

'Bad dreams?' she asked.

'Could be.'

'Nightmare on Elm Park?'

'Something like that.'

'So I gathered. You were talking in your sleep
last night.'

'Last night? What day is this then?'

'Monday.'

'Jesus, what happened to Sunday?'

'A winter's Sunday in Brixton Hill? You were
lucky to miss it. I let you sleep through.'

'What time is it?'

'Seven-thirty.'

'In the morning?'

'Got it in one.'

'I haven't slept properly for a few days.'

'It showed. You look better for some rest.'

I didn't think I could have looked much worse.

'Thanks for the hospitality.'

'Just as well I didn't have a boyfriend in.'

'I didn't know you had a boyfriend. I thought you were saving yourself for me.'

'If I was you'd have to grow up a bit, and I don't think I can wait that long.'

'Aren't I mature enough for you, then?'

'Mature, you? Mentally you haven't reached the age of consent.'

I guessed she was right. Having no responsibilities means someone else always looking after your arse and getting you out of trouble. So I changed the subject. That one was a bit too close to home.

'Did you sleep with me?'

'Of course. There's only one bed.'

'Did I, *you know*?'

'You tried, but you couldn't get it up.'

'That's nothing new. It runs in the family. I hope I didn't get you too hot.'

She gave me a disgusted look. 'I didn't have to bite my knuckles in frustration, if that's what you mean.'

'That's OK then. Maybe next time.'

'Maybe.'

'I'll dream about it.'

'Dream on.'

'Now *you're* getting *me* hot.'

'Your mind is like a sewer.'

'My mind is OK, it's my armpits that are like sewers.'

'Want a bath?'

'Good idea.'

'I'll run one.'

'Hot,' I said.

'As hot as you can handle.'

The way I felt, that wouldn't be very hot at all. I struggled out of bed and wrapped myself in a sheet.

'Modest too,' said Wanda.

I felt another crash coming. 'Wanda,' I said, and my voice sounded miles away and I nearly fell. She supported me, and held me tightly.

'Are you all right?'

'I'll manage. I've been pushing the boat out a bit over the past few days.'

'I would never have guessed.'

'It's not what you think.'

'If you say so. By the way, how's your leg?'

'I'll survive.'

'You're not taking care of it, and your foot's swollen. I had a terrible job getting that boot and sock off. Why aren't you using your stick?'

'I lost it.'

'You're a bloody fool to yourself.'

'I know, but I'll be OK. I've just got to take care of a little business. Then the scars can harden or else it won't matter.'

'You can't leave. You're not well enough.'

'I've got to.'

She tightened her mouth but didn't argue. I followed her into the bathroom like a dog. As I went in she stalked out and slammed the door. I shrugged.

The bathroom smelled fragrant and both taps were gushing into a green, scented bubble bath. I turned off the cold tap and tested the water. Perfect. I dropped the sheet and eased myself into the water with a groan. I looked at my leg. It had the texture and colour of raw meat and my left foot had swollen by at least a size and a half. I hoped that I would be able to get my boot back on.

I soaked for an hour, adding scalding water as required. I got out when my skin began to crinkle. There were hot towels on the rail. As I reached for one I crashed badly again. I felt dizzy and sick, and the room tilted and went grey and misty at the edges. Familiar items looked mysterious. I sat on a towel on the closed toilet seat and put my head between my knees. I closed my eyes and saw stars on a black background. Sweat popped out of my body and I gripped my calves and breathed deeply. Jesus, if this went on I was going to have to think about changing my lifestyle.

I felt wet hair on my bare thighs and pressed my eyelids hard into my eyeballs and put my head back on to the cool plastic of the cistern. There was a knock on the door. I modestly covered myself – every man does, take my word – and said, 'Yes?'

Wanda stuck her head round the door and asked, 'Are you OK?'

'Sure, why?'

'You've been in there such a long time.'

'I'm good.'

'I never noticed.'

'Gee, thanks, Wanda. After that kind of compliment I'll be right on top today.'

She stuck out her tongue. 'Are you sure you'll be OK? You look as white as a sheet.'

'Just a bad moment.'

'How bad is it?'

'I'll survive.'

'Will you be all right on your own?'

I smiled, and it hurt. 'I'll be fine,' I said, and wondered who I was trying to convince. Her or me.

I finished drying myself and wrapped a towel around my waist – I went looking for Wanda. She was sitting at the kitchen table sipping at a china mug of tea and looking at yesterday's *Observer*. She got up and got me a mug of my own. I sat down opposite her and pinched one of her B&H.

'Want something to eat?' she asked.

'Good idea.'

'Bacon and eggs?'

I tasted curry again. 'Just eggs,' I said quickly. 'Egg and chips would be good.'

She looked at me strangely, she had fed me before, but 'No problem,' was all she said. 'Your clothes are in the airing cupboard,' she added.

I went and found them and dressed in everything but my DMs. I thought I'd cross that bridge when I came to it. Wanda had washed and ironed everything.

I went back to the kitchen which was warm and cosy with cooking smells. 'Thanks for doing my laundry.'

'I had to, they stank.'

'I'm not surprised.'

I sat down at the table. It had been laid with a bright cloth, a knife and fork and ketchup and salt.

She brought me the food, then sat down with another mug of tea.

'So what happened?'

'I thought you'd never ask.'

'That means don't ask, right?'

'Right.'

'But I'm curious.'

'Curiosity killed The Cat Woman.'

'That bad?'

'For me.'

'And you won't tell me?'

'It's a long story. Too long. I can't even work it out myself. I've just been taken for a mug by a whole bunch of people.'

'And that will never do.'

'It's cost lives.'

She turned white. 'You're joking.'

'I wish I was.'

'Did you . . . ?'

'No.'

'Who, then?'

'I'll tell you all about it later. It'll be over soon, one way or another.'

'Stay here.'

'I can't.'

'Please.'

'I wish I could. It would be easier.'

'Sod you then.'

'Don't be like that.'

'A man's gotta do,' she said sarcastically.

'Funny, I said much the same the other day myself. Strange how we all talk in clichés, isn't it? Will you give me a lift later?'

'Nick, it's not a good idea. You're in no condition.'

'Forget that. Will you give me a lift or not?'

She gave in all of a sudden. 'You can have the bloody car if you like.'

Her car was a Morris Minor 1000 traveller, circa 1955 with a dodgy transmission and bald tyres.

'No. Thanks all the same. A ride will be fine.'

'Where do you want to go?'

'Waterloo.'

'What's in Waterloo?'

'Who,' I corrected her.

'Who then?'

'Someone I know. Someone I have to see.'

'A woman?'

I nodded.

'Why?'

'I have to let her know I'm all right.'

Wanda pursed her lips but didn't speak.

I ate the eggs and chips, and a tin of beans and some toast, and drank three cups of tea in silence. Hers as much as mine. I felt like a jerk treating Wanda so badly, but it was the only way I could protect her.

Finally I faced up to my boots. The right one was OK, but the left felt like a vice on my foot. I survived.

Before we left she asked me if I wanted to see my cat that she had been looking after for longer than I cared to remember.

'Sure,' I said.

She took me into a back room where a big black and white moggie was lording it over a couple of smaller cats.

'Is that him?' I asked. 'Christ, he's grown. Do you think he'll remember me?'

'I doubt it. You don't feed him.'

'A man and his cat never forget.' Cat looked at me suspiciously but came and sniffed my fingers and let me pet him. 'See,' I said, and he turned and spat at me. 'Just like his old mum,' I said proudly.

'Are you ever going to accept your responsibilities for anything?' asked Wanda. I heard tears in her voice. That one struck home. It referred back too accurately to my own earlier thoughts.

'Let's go,' I said.

We went outside to where the Morris waited, and shoved hardened snow dotted with little specks of soot off the bodywork and on to the street. The old starter motor turned the engine over half a dozen times to no avail, and I could just begin to hear the battery beginning to lose power when the engine caught. Wanda pumped gas and the exhaust belched, missed, and belched again before the engine roared healthily.

Wanda adjusted the choke and looked over at me. 'Good old car,' she said.

'Keep the revs up and for Christ's sake turn on the heater, I'm freezing,' I said. She did as she was told and the engine settled to a lumpy idle while warmish air crept into the cab. When everything seemed safe, I agreed with her. 'Good old car,' I echoed, and she smiled despite herself.

It was just after ten when we pulled away from the kerb, leaving an icy bare patch on the roadside.

Wanda headed towards town and within twenty minutes or so I directed her around to the row of pre-fabs close to Waterloo Station.

The little box of a house looked like an illustration on a Christmas card, with icicles hanging down from the trellis over the door and the flat roof covered in snow, except where heat from the chimney had melted a circle of moisture about a yard in diameter.

'Who lives here?' Wanda asked. 'The seven dwarves or just Snow White?'

'Don't be like that, Wanda.'

'How should I be?'

'A friend, just be a friend.'

And of course she had been, and it was an insult for me to suggest otherwise, but 'All right, Nick' was all she said, an edge of sadness in her voice that I'll never forget.

'Thanks, Wanda. I owe you one.'

'I'll wait if you like.'

'No, it's OK. You get on home. I'll be in touch.'

'Are you sure?'

'Sure.'

'What happens if she isn't here?'

'I'll think of something.'

She shrugged and sighed, but let me go.

22

I got out of the Morris. It pulled away with a crash of gears, a clunk from the engine and much dark smoke from the exhaust pipe. I didn't see Wanda again for a lifetime, but that's another story.

I lifted my hand to the retreating car as it turned into the main road past the hospital, but there was no acknowledgement.

I walked across the snowy street and up the freshly swept front path to the door of the pre-fab. My head was clear but my leg and foot were on fire and I hoped that I was doing myself no permanent damage.

I stood on the small porch and thumbed the door-bell. I heard the faint sound of ringing from indoors as I huddled inside my jacket for warmth, and waited.

A middle-aged man in a wheelchair answered the door. He was whippet thin, with long shaggy hair and a full, grizzled beard. He sat in the doorway and looked at me, I stood on the porch and looked back. 'Is Fiona in?' I asked.

'Are you Sharman?'

I nodded.

'We've been waiting for you. She's told me all about you. Funny, I expected someone younger.'

I ignored the veiled insult. 'Is she here?' I said.
'Yes.'

I stood there on the doorstep like a milk bottle.
'Come on in then,' the man said, wheeling himself
back and allowing the door to open a little wider.
'All the heat's getting out.'

I edged through the gap and shut the door behind
me, standing awkwardly in the narrow hall. It was
warm and smelt of furniture polish and clean
laundry. The inside of the house was tiny and neat.
A hallway ran from front to back, with two doors to
the left, three to the right. At the end of the hall was
a half glass door leading to the back garden.

'I'm Stan,' he said. 'Her dad.' I shook his hand. It
was like holding a handful of hinged steel tightly
wrapped in warm leather.

'She talks about you too,' I said.

'Nothing good, I hope.' He dropped my hand and
spun the chair round on its axis. 'She's in there,'
he said, pointing to the second door on the left. 'Go
on in.'

I did as I was told. Fiona was sitting in an armchair by a tiny open grate that glowed hot with
smokeless fuel. She was wearing jeans and a
sweater, and her hair was tied back in bunches.
She looked up, then looked again. 'Nick, *at last*. I've
been out of my mind. Where have you been?'

'Around,' I said.

'The police are at your flat. They're looking
for you.'

'I can imagine.'

'It's been on the news and in this morning's
papers.' She gestured to a pile of newsprint on the
floor. It looked like she'd bought the shop.

'Let's have a look,' I said.

She passed me the top paper. It was the *Express*, not my usual choice of reading matter, but this wasn't a usual day.

'Get him some tea, Fiona,' said Stan. 'He looks like he could use a cup.' Obediently she left the room. I reminded myself to ask him how he did it. I could hear her clattering about in the kitchen whilst I looked at the paper. I sat down in the armchair she had vacated, and moved it so that my bad leg got the benefit of the heat.

The story was on page four. It wasn't very big, only two people died after all. There had been an earthquake in China over the weekend, 25,000 deceased and still counting. My little epic was very small beer compared to that.

PRIVATE EYE SOUGHT IN LONDON MURDER HUNT

Police are today searching for Nicholas Sharman (38), an ex-Metropolitan police officer and private detective, in connection with a bizarre double murder in South London on Saturday night. The body of Lawrence Taylor (42) and an unidentified woman were found in a flat in Kennington early on Sunday morning after an anonymous telephone call to Scotland Yard. Police entered the flat and found the pair who had apparently been tortured before being killed. Taylor, an officer in the department of Customs & Excise, lived in Eastleigh, near Southampton with his wife Veronica (36). She was not available for comment at their luxury £250,000 detached house last night.

It is believed that Taylor was the officer in charge of a store of contraband drugs, and reports that a large, although yet unspecified amount of drugs are missing from the store were denied by senior customs officials today.

Sharman, a shadowy figure with known drug and underworld connections has been linked to a number of spectacular crimes in the past few years, including the deaths of music business moguls Charles and Steven Diva and the strange case of media supremo Sir Robert Pike's bogus daughter.

A Scotland Yard spokesman said last night: "Sharman is well known in the area and we expect to interview him within the next twenty-four hours. However, anyone with any knowledge of his whereabouts should contact us immediately."

All that meant was, the Scotland Yard spokesman didn't know where I was or what the fuck was going on, except I was on the 'Most Wanted' list. But at least the news item told me who the mysterious Lawrence Taylor was, or rather had been, a customs man in charge of the evidence cupboard. It was like a replay of my life and I felt chilled to the bone. It was all dropping into place, one piece after another. I riffled through the other papers. They all said much the same in slightly different words.

As I finished, Fiona came back balancing a tray with three mugs, a teapot, a jug of milk, a pot of sugar and a couple of spoons on it.

I took my tea and she said, 'Come on, Sharman for Christ's sake, what's happening?'

'They got my age wrong,' I said.

'Be serious.'

So I was, and I told them. Everything since I'd dropped Fiona off two nights previously. Everything including what I'd found at the flat in Kennington, and as I told them about that I smelt cooking meat again and put the tea down and lit a cigarette.

'Why didn't you come straight here?' demanded Fiona.

'I got away on a bus, and it wasn't going in this direction.'

'A bus, eh?' said Stan. 'Desperado.'

Fiona flashed him a dirty look. 'So where have you been?' she asked.

'At a friend's.'

'What friend?'

'Just a friend. Does it matter?'

It obviously did, but what could I do?

'Doesn't your *friend* have a television? How come you didn't know that you were all over the news? Were you too busy?'

'I slept the clock round,' I said. 'I was dead. And, no, as a matter of fact she doesn't have a television.'

'*She*, I knew it!' said Fiona, and threw herself down in a two-seater sofa, her face as black as thunder.

Shit, I thought.

Her father looked from her to me and back, and pulled a face. That was when I started to like him. I pulled a face back. He propelled his wheelchair towards me and helped himself to one of my cigarettes. 'Why do you think this character Taylor telephoned you?' he asked.

'Who knows?' I said. 'Maybe he got an attack of the guilts and wanted to come clean. I'm not the police. Perhaps he thought he could talk to me and I'd help him. Maybe he had a gun at his head and whoever was holding it wanted me too. But I promise I'll find out.'

'So you think he was supplying Watkins with cocaine that had already been confiscated and that he liberated from the store he was in charge of?'

'I think he was supplying, full stop,' I said. 'And it's pretty obvious that Teddy was making the pick-up, but Emerald knew nothing about it. I still believe that. If he knew, he wouldn't be in Brixton now. He'd be long gone. The only thing that doesn't make sense is why Teddy left the dope there when Emerald had been tipped off about the bust, and Teddy knew the lock-up was on the Bill's hit list.'

'Maybe he didn't,' said Stan.

'Come again?'

'Maybe Taylor was making a delivery and Teddy got cold feet waiting, knowing the fuzz were on the way.'

'That's it, Stan,' I said. 'Of course. And Taylor didn't know what was happening and left the stuff, and the law found it.'

'But who tipped off the law in the first place?' asked Stan.

My head was beginning to hurt. 'Christ knows,' I said. 'That's another thing I intend to find out.'

'Go to the police then,' said Fiona, her sulks forgotten.

'Talk sense,' I said. 'You read what it said in the paper. My name's right in the frame for this one. They've already got Emerald banged up on remand. They'd love to have me there too, and on a double murder charge. You didn't see those people. Whoever did it was a psycho. I will go to the police, but not until I've got all the answers to the questions they're going to ask me, and can prove that it's Teddy and whoever's behind him that they really want.'

'You don't think he's doing it on his own?' asked Stan.

I shook my head. 'Whatever he is, he's not capable of doing what was done on Saturday night, and certainly not alone. I'll lay money that he'd never been to that flat before he went in with me.'

'Tell the police that,' said Fiona.

'They won't believe me, and he could be anywhere by now. This is my old game, why I left the force in the first place. *Déjà vu*, if you like. There's a couple of detectives I know who'll lose the key if I turn myself in now. I'm seriously fucked, and the only one who can get me out of it is me.'

'So what are you going to do?'

'I'm going to go looking for them, starting with Jack Dark. At least I've got an address for him. He's dirty that man, very dirty. Whatever those two in Kennington were up to, they didn't deserve to end up the way they did. Someone wants me to carry the can for it, and I won't. I think Dark's the man, or knows who is.'

'I'm going with you,' she said.

'No.'

'Yes, you're not going to vanish on me again. The only woman friend you're going to be with is me.'

I looked at her father. He shrugged. He knew her better than I did. 'I'd go with you myself if it wasn't for these damn things,' he said, and slapped one of his dead legs.

I gave in, I was past arguing. 'All right,' I said. 'But we'll need a car.'

'There's mine,' she said. 'I went and got it yesterday. I had to dig it out. That's when I saw the police at your place. It's parked around the corner under the bridge, out of the way.'

'Do behave, Fiona,' I said. 'It hasn't even got a bloody roof, and it's freezing out and we're going to Essex. God knows what the weather's like there. What we really need is four-wheel drive. Teddy's little motor would have been ideal.'

'I suppose you're right,' she said. 'It was full of snow when I got it. I never thought of that.'

I looked towards the heavens. 'I'll get you one,' said Stan.

'Do what?'

'I'll get you one. I've got a mate.'

I looked from him to Fiona, who nodded. 'Go on then,' I said.

He wheeled over to the table that held the phone, and punched out a number. He whispered something, listened, whispered again and put the receiver down. 'It'll be here in an hour,' he said.

'A straight car,' I said.

'Sure.'

'With four-wheel drive?'

'Sure.'

'Just like that, nothing to pay?'

'Sure.'

'I'll need a weapon too.'

'I'll get you one.'

'You've got a mate?'

'Better than that,' he said. 'I wasn't in the service of Queen and country for nothing.' He pushed himself over to the corner of the room and pulled back the carpet to reveal a metal door, fitted flush with the concrete floor. He took a set of keys from his shirt pocket, bent over the arm of his chair and used what looked like a Chubb to open the lock. He turned the key both ways then pulled. The door opened smoothly on counter weights, up and across to give maximum space below. Stan reached in and pulled out a stripped down, single-barrelled, pistol-gripped shotgun from the recess. 'Winchester twelve gauge,' he said. 'Magnum. I'll give you a lend of this, if you can handle it.'

'I'll do my best,' I said. 'Got a sling or something for it?'

'Somewhere.'

'Fine.'

Stan reached in again and took out a small pine box. He snapped the brass catch on the front and opened it. On purple velvet lay the blued steel of a small calibre automatic, well used but clean and oiled.

He tossed it to Fiona who caught it expertly and checked the clip. 'Keep it handy, love,' said Stan. 'And remember what I taught you.'

'Ammunition?' I asked.

Stan bent down again. He reached into the hole and came out with a cardboard box. He fished out a shotgun shell and flipped it in my direction. I caught it and shook it close by my ear. The red cardboard tube sounded like it was full of marbles. I looked at Stan.

'Ball bearings,' he said. 'A dozen or so to a load. A couple of those will take the side off a Transit van.'

'How many does this thing hold?' I asked.

'Five.'

'That'll do.'

He counted out four more shells and brought them to me. I lined them up on the arm of my chair, like little soldiers waiting to go into battle, then cleared the action of the gun. It sounded sweet and true and I checked that the barrel was clear. I dry fired a few times and the pull was good and clean. When I was happy I loaded it. Each of the five shells slid home with a satisfying snick.

'I'm going to wash up the dishes,' said Stan, and expertly gathered up the dirty mugs and balanced the tray on his knee and left the room. Fiona came over and perched on my knee and ground her backside into my crotch. 'Did you sleep with someone else?'

'I cannot tell a lie – no,' I lied. Well, I didn't really. I hadn't known what I was doing. And apparently I couldn't anyway, according to Wanda. At least that was how I justified it to myself.

'Come with me then,' she whispered in my ear.

'Where?'

'In the other room.'

'Why?'

'Don't ask questions, just come with me.'

I followed her and she took me across the hall into a small bedroom. It was colder in there and smelt of her perfume. 'What do you want?' I asked.

'You're dim sometimes, Sharman, you know that?' she said, and pulled her sweater over her head and undid her blue jeans and let them fall and kicked them away. Underneath she was wearing plain white cotton underwear. Nothing fancy or particularly sexy but it got to me. She was wearing thick white socks too. And it could have been comical, but it wasn't. If you want to know it was as erotic as hell. She saw me looking and put her hand on the wall for support, lifting first one foot and then the other to peel the socks off. I tugged off my shirt and went to her in the chilly room. I kissed her and held her hot little body close to mine. The curtains were half drawn and the snow outside reflected the light on to the solid planes of her body and lit and shaded her skin with its glow.

Her mouth smelled of tea and cigarettes and I licked her lips with my tongue. We staggered and fell on to the narrow bed. I pushed her bra up above her breasts and bit at her nipples. She sighed long and hard and I pushed her pants over her hips and down until she could kick them free. She pulled at my trousers and I pushed them and my shorts off together. I remembered my socks too. I mounted her on the narrow bed. She was soft and wet against my hardness. She came almost immediately. I did too.

'Good,' she said. That was all and we kissed again. I'll never forget the look on her face in the soft light or the feel of her mouth slithering over mine.

We lay on top of the covers for a few minutes, holding each other. 'Pass us me pants, Sharman,' she said eventually. 'I'm leaking. I've got to go to the loo.'

I did. She went. It got colder without her.

I got up and put my clothes back on. I was missing a button from my shirt. I went out into the corridor and Fiona was in the kitchen helping Stan with the drying up. I saw her through the half-opened door. I went and talked to them. We didn't talk about where we were going.

The car arrived on the hour as promised. It was a Sierra 4x4, white as it happened, which was fine by me as it wouldn't stand out in the snow if we had to hang around Emerson Park for long. The guy who delivered it said little and took a twenty for cab fare. We didn't have to sign any papers and I didn't ask where it had come from.

Stan found a webbing strap with clips at each end that mated with the rings welded to the barrel and grip of the riot gun. I adjusted the strap and hung the Winchester over my right shoulder. Fiona found me an old trench coat. It was greasy and creased and matched my mood exactly. I put it on over the Winchester. The open poacher pockets allowed me to hold the weapon down beneath the coat, close to my leg, and get it up and ready to fire in a second. It could make a mess of the material, but *c'est la guerre*.

Fiona went out and filled up the car with petrol. She checked the oil and tyres and brought it back. We left. Stan waved from the doorway and I waved back.

23

Fiona drove. I didn't want to use a clutch with my
leg. She'd done a bit of packing before we left and
there was a canvas holdall on the back seat. Next
to it was a cheap black baseball cap with *Ford*
picked out on the front in pale blue thread. I put it
on and pulled the peak down over my eyes. 'Very
stylish,' she said.

'It'll do,' I said back.

She pulled the Sierra into Lambeth Palace Road
and headed east. We drove down York Road,
round the roundabout and down Stamford Street.
The roads were fairly clear that close to the centre
of town and we made good time.

As we drove I opened the holdall and examined
the contents. On top were two down-filled sleeping
bags. A depressing thought, but the nights were
cold. Underneath the bags were the goodies. A half
bottle of Smirnoff, a flask of coffee and a loaf of
bread made up into sandwiches and wrapped in
silver foil, a handful of ready rolled joints in a
tobacco tin, and a dozen Duromine from Fiona's
bathroom stash. I held a tab of speed between my
finger and thumb. 'Want some?' I asked.

She looked at me and grinned. 'Do you think we'll
need them?'

'We're on the run, girl,' I said. 'And you're with a bad motherfucker. Worse still, everyone's after us – the bad guys and the good. I think we'll definitely need something.'

'All right,' she said. 'But they're murder on my complexion.'

I didn't comment. After what I'd seen, I knew there were worse things. I gave her two of the pills. 'Want some vodka to wash them down?'

'Go on then.'

I broke the seal on the new bottle, unscrewed the top and passed it to her. She swallowed the pills, took a hit and pulled a face. 'Wicked,' she said. I took the bottle back and did the same myself. The spirit was warm and I almost gagged. I put the other pills in with the joints and hid the tin in the glove compartment.

We stopped at the lights on the south side of London Bridge and a Panda car pulled up on the inside.

'Shit,' I said.

'It's all right,' said Fiona. 'I'll beat him out easy in this.'

I pulled the shotgun up on to my lap and slipped the safety. 'You won't have to,' I said. 'If they get nosy, I'll blow the front off that son of a bitch.' The cop at the wheel glanced round at me, then to the front, then at me again. I nodded politely and he nodded back. My stomach was in a knot as the lights changed and the police car pulled in front of us and its brake lights flared. 'Fuck it,' I spat through gritted teeth, and pumped a cartridge full of ball bearings that would not only take the front off the son of a bitch but maybe the legs off the son

214

of a bitch who was driving it as well, into the breech of the shotgun. The blue lamp on top of the car spun slowly, then faster, and my hands were slippery on the action of the Winchester. The Panda's siren yipped and it indicated right and took off down a side street to parts unknown. I relaxed and blew out my breath. I felt sweat trickling down from my armpits and dampening my shirt.

'Let's go to Essex.'

The journey would have been a nightmare without the four-wheel drive on the Sierra. The roads had been gritted but were slick with melted snow, and icy water sometimes lay inches deep on the surface. Black spray from other vehicles covered our car and the windscreen was thick with a mixture of sand, salt, mud and water which had the consistency of glue. The windscreen wipers were finding it hard to cope. Sensibly, Fiona had checked the reservoir bottle before we set off that morning, but we still had to stop at a garage on Ripple Road when the nozzles for the washer got blocked up with dirt or ice just past Newham. To help the flow she added anti-freeze to the washer bottle and I thought that whoever *did* own the Sierra wouldn't thank us, but that's the way of the world. Whilst Fiona was fiddling about under the bonnet I found a telephone box and called Jack Dark's home number. I let the phone ring twenty times before I hung up.

We pressed on and eventually saw signs for Hornchurch. We came off the A13 and got to Little Beverly Hills about four. It was already dark and the temperature was dropping again. We drove around the snowy, tree-lined avenues for what seemed like hours, looking for the address on the card I'd taken from Jack Dark. It's real swanky up there if your idea of swanky is a swimming pool, a rotating satellite dish in the back garden, a stone sphinx on the front lawn, frou-frou nylon net curtains and a professional footballer for a next-door neighbour. Personally, I'd rather live in Beirut.

'I had a boyfriend lived here once,' said Fiona as she pointed the car down yet another broad boulevard.

'He didn't live *here*, did he?' I asked, reading out the street name on the card.

'No, but he used to take me to a smashing disco in Romford.'

'Don't tell me, the Hollywood,' I said.

'Do you know it?'

'No, but I've heard of it. Did he drive an XR3i cabriolet?'

'That's right, an electric blue one. His name's Joey Harris. Do you know him?'

'No, but I know the type.'

'Are you jealous?'

'There's not a jealous bone in my body, Fiona.'

'I believe you, you uptight bastard.'

We drove around some more and kept squinting out for road signs. If there were any they were covered in snow and invisible. It seemed that nobody walked in Emerson Park. The streets were deserted. Finally we fell in behind a nearly new Peugeot 205 which must have been low car on the totem pole in the area. It indicated and pulled up on a snow-covered drive. I told Fiona to stop, and gave her the card with Jack Dark's address. She went

over to inquire of the driver. She picked her way
daintily across the road, through the ice. A young
blonde woman got out of the Peugeot and Fiona
spoke to her briefly. The woman pointed in the
direction we were heading and said something to
Fiona I couldn't hear. She came back and got behind
the wheel, bringing a blast of frigid air in with her.
'Christ, but it's cold out there.'

'Well?'

'Left and left again.'

'Great, let's go.'

Fiona put the Sierra into gear and we slid along
the icy road.

The woman had been right. When we had followed her simple directions, I finally found a street
sign and cleared off the snow and we were there.
Fiona drove the car slowly down the street and we
found the house.

It was much as I'd expected – a sprawling,
ranch-style residence built on a good-sized piece of
land that sloped upwards away from the road
towards the tree line and God knows what beyond.
It was dark up there. The snow covered the drive
and garden, and as far as I could see no cars had
been or gone since the last heavy fall. Only a few
footprints broke the path to the front door and snow
had drifted steeply against the triple garage door.
The house was dark. Even the fairy lights on the
Christmas tree close to the front porch were off.

'No one home again,' I said.

'Someone's been to the door,' said Fiona.

'Just single tracks, postman I'll bet. The front
door hasn't been opened. There's snow piled up
against it, see.'

'Where do you think they are?'

'Who knows? Looks like he's taken his family and buggered off.'

'Do you think he'll be back?'

'Eventually, maybe tonight, but Christ knows when. And we can't wait here. It's too bloody cold and the neighbours will call the police if we hang around the streets too long. I don't want to go back to town. If we push on a bit we're bound to find somewhere to stay. I don't fancy sleeping rough tonight, even with sleeping bags.'

'Do you think it'll be safe?'

'We've got to take a chance. Have you got plastic?'

She nodded.

'Good,' I said. 'I can't use mine. That's taking too much of a chance. Let's go. Head away from London.'

Fiona started the car and we drove out of Emerson Park and along some minor roads until we joined the A12. We found a motel on a roundabout near Pilgrim's Hatch, wherever that is. There was a sign outside that said VACANCIES in blue neon.

'You check in,' I said. 'I'll carry the bag and stay back. If anyone says anything tell them we're on our way to Colchester and you don't like the look of the weather and we decided to stop off for the night. OK.'

'OK,' she said.

I took hold of the bag, pulled my cap down over my eyes and followed her into the reception area. It smelled of nylon carpet and warmed-over food like all cheap hotels. But it was warm and we needed the shelter.

Fiona marched across to the desk and plonked down her handbag. There was only one receptionist on duty, a middle-aged woman with a too youthful hairstyle and a white blouse under a navy blue cardigan. She looked up as Fiona approached.

'Yes dear?' she said in a pleasant voice.

'You've got some vacancies?' asked Fiona.

'Yes, a few.'

'Thank goodness. I thought we'd have to keep driving and the roads are awful, and it looks like it could snow again soon.'

Don't overdo it, I thought.

'I know, dear,' said the woman. 'We've had some cancellations, so you're lucky.'

'Have you got a double room?'

The woman looked over at me. 'Of course. Are you going far?'

'Colchester,' said Fiona. 'But we're in no rush. So we decided to stop off overnight and carry on tomorrow. Perhaps the weather will have improved.'

'It might,' said the woman. 'But I doubt it.'

'We'd still rather drive in daylight.'

'Of course. I always say it's safer.' The woman looked away from me and told Fiona the rates for a double room with en-suite bath. And told her, yes, we could eat in our room and took the details of her credit card and gave her a key. 'It's one of our best rooms,' she said. 'Just down the corridor, away from the public rooms, so it's nice and quiet.'

'Thank you,' said Fiona and I followed her, and nodded politely to the receptionist and hoped she'd forget all about us.

We found the room and Fiona let us in. It was

nondescript, just like a million other hotel rooms in the world with a small double bed, a TV, a long, wall-mounted unit, on top of which was a plastic folder with a room service menu and writing paper and envelopes inside, plus a tourist guide to places of local interest. Next to the folder was an electric kettle and a tray holding a bowl of tea bags and sachets of coffee, sugar and little containers of long-life milk, two cups, saucers and spoons. Above the unit was a mirror with wall lamps on either side. Half of the wall opposite was taken up by a fitted wardrobe. In the other half was another door leading to a tiny bathroom. I dropped the bag on to the bed and took off my coat and hung it on the chair and put the shotgun in the wardrobe.

'Tea?' I asked.

'Love one,' said Fiona.

I filled up the kettle in the bathroom and plugged it in and put on the TV with the sound down. The news was on, but I didn't feature. I *was* on the local news, but right at the end and the photo they showed did me no justice, but I hoped the receptionist didn't catch it anyway.

'Christ!' said Fiona. 'What happens if someone recognises you?'

'It's a chance we've got to take, babe,' I said. 'We couldn't have stayed out all night in this weather, we'd have frozen. No one's going to recognise me from that poxy picture.'

'I hope you're right.'

'So do I. But I'll keep out of sight when the food comes.'

'Shall I order something?' she asked. 'I'm starving.'

'Do it. I'm going to have a bath.' I went into the bathroom and started the taps. When the bath was full and the water felt right I got in. It felt good on my leg. I lay there until Fiona came in.

'The food'll be here in half an hour. I ordered roast beef. Is that OK?'

'Sounds good. Did you get anything to drink?'

'A bottle of wine.'

'You're as good as gold,' I said.

'Sure. Now stay here until the food comes. I'll give you a shout.'

I did as I was told.

About twenty minutes later I heard voices in the room and I got out of the bath and towelled myself dry and started to get dressed. As I was buttoning my shirt, Fiona stuck her head round the door.

'Dinner.'

'I'm with you.'

She'd laid out the food and drink on the table. The beef was surprisingly good and we cleared our plates and drank all but the dregs of the bottle of wine. After dinner we smoked a joint and went to bed and made love. But neither of us had our heart in it.

I watched myself on the news again after the ten o'clock bulletin. This time my photo was only on for a second and I doubted if anyone would recognise me from its brief appearance. We smoked another joint and went back to bed to sleep. I couldn't, and lay awake most of the night looking at the ceiling.

I woke Fiona early and she took a bath and we had breakfast, but neither of us had much of an appetite. She went and settled the bill and I stayed in the room and we left. Before we went I took a tab of speed. It was getting to be a habit. There was a man on reception then. He didn't even bother to look at me. We drove back to Emerson Park. We were there by nine. There was no more sign of life at the Darks' than there had been the previous evening. I looked at the houses on either side. The one on the right had a light on behind the bullseye glass in the front door and another behind the huge picture window to the left of the porch. 'Give them a knock, sweetheart,' I said. 'Ask them if they know where the Darks are. Tell them you're a friend of one of the daughters.'

'What are the daughters' names?'

'I don't know, busk it. Use your charm.'

She pulled the rearview mirror round and examined her face in it. 'I don't feel very charming,' she said. 'I look a mess.'

'You look beautiful.'

'Liar.'

'I mean it.'

'I believe you, thousands wouldn't.'

She left the engine of the Sierra running so that I could keep the heater on, got out of the car and walked across to the house and rang the bell. It opened after a minute but I couldn't see who answered it from where I was sitting. Fiona was talking and pointing at the Darks' house, and after thirty seconds or so she went inside. She didn't come out for fifteen minutes, and when she did she waved as if she'd been visiting old friends. She slithered down the drive and back to the car. 'Well?' I asked.

'I had coffee and biscuits,' she replied. 'I sat in the

kitchen with Kathy, she lives there, and had a nice chat.'

'Good for you, and for Kathy. I hope it was fresh coffee. Where's Dark?'

'Visiting relatives. Kathy's looking after the youngest daughter's hamster.'

'Very good. When will they be back?'

'They won't, not this side of Christmas. The whole family's going to Marbella on Christmas Eve. They always go away for Christmas.'

'Last year it was St Lucia,' I said. 'Marbella, eh? I think Kathy may have to adopt that hamster.'

'What do you mean?'

'I mean Dark's got the shits. When did they go, do you know?'

'It was sudden, on Sunday.'

'I bet it was! He knew I'd got away and had his address. They won't be back.

'We're going at this from the wrong end,' I said after a while.

'How do you mean?'

'I mean that if we want to find out where the coke's being wholesaled, we need to start where it's retailed.'

'Where's that?'

'Back in town. I know a geezer who'll put us right – or I'll rip his head off.'

24

There are half a dozen pubs round Stockwell that I
definitely wouldn't recommend for a family outing.
Hard pubs where strangers are not welcome. But
they were the boozers where Malteser hung out, so
that's where we had to go. Malteser is a slippery
little Brother with processed hair and little glasses
and a craving for coke that was something to be
near. I could have busted him any number of times
when I was on the force, but he was only a user so I
never bothered. I reckoned he owed me one for old
times' sake.

Fiona and I dumped the Sierra on a parking
meter in a back street off Stockwell Road around
noon. Before we got out of the car I put the baseball cap on again and pulled it right down over
my face and turned the collar of the trench coat
up until they almost met. 'Listen, sweetheart,' I
said to her, 'I'm well known round here, too well
known, and I'm not popular. Also I'm wanted, and
there's a good few would be happy to turn me in,
to either side. So I'm expecting you to watch my
back.'

She tapped her handbag. 'It's all right,
Sharman. I'm ready.'

'Can you use that thing?'

'Don't be daft. My old man won at Bisley. I inherited his eye.'

I didn't argue. It would have been pointless. We'd come too far together for that.

Malteser was sitting in the snug of the third German we tried. At least it said SNUG on the door in old-fashioned script. Inside it was anything but. It was a freezing room with a broken gas fire and worn lino on the floor. Malteser was sitting with two debutantes you wouldn't take home to Mother's unless Mother was on a six-week cruise and you had the place to yourself. The furniture in the bar consisted of two wooden-topped tables and half a dozen chairs, a couple of speakers hooked up to the juke box in the saloon bar and a pay telephone on the wall that was defaced with phone numbers and decorated with dozens of mini-cab firm cards fixed to the wall with drawing pins. Malteser and the two debs were alone at one table drinking Red Stripe out of cans.

I pulled out a couple of chairs from the other. Fiona sat on one, her handbag open on her lap. I asked her if she wanted a drink. She declined. I went to the bar and hollered, and an old dear who'd been nattering in the public came round the bar and poured me a large Jack Daniel's.

I took it back to the table and sat down. The barrel of the shotgun stuck through the material of my coat like a giant erection. Deb number one checked it out. I checked her out. She was a big girl with nappy hair dyed crimson, half a ton of cheap slap on her boat race, black, skin-tight cycling vest and shorts with a yellow stripe up the side under a fox fur coat, an ankle chain with a gold cross attached and red plastic spike-heeled shoes. Real class.

I didn't want the women around, just Malteser. 'What do you say, man?' I said.

'Mellow-D.'

'Get rid of your girlfriends, there's a love.'

'You talking about us?' asks deb number two, who was wearing thigh-length boots with hot pants, a see-through white blouse with a black bra underneath, and a pair of wire-rimmed spectacles. She looked a bit like Janet Jackson on magic mushrooms. Old magic mushrooms.

I took a deep pull of my drink. 'Has anyone ever told you you look like Janet Jackson?'

'All the time,' she simpered, and touched her bins with a handful of bitten-to-the-quick fingernails.

'They're lying. Now get out of here, both of you. Half the day gone already, and not a penny earned.'

'Sez you,' said deb number one.

I gave them a twenty each and they left. All that remained of them was the smell of too much cheap perfume.

'I been hearing things about you, Nick,' said Malteser when the door to the saloon had closed behind them.

'Like what?'

'Like you been a naughty boy, and consequently you been moving round.'

'Yes, Malteser,' I said. 'I'm moving round, and it's Mr Sharman to you. Always was, always will be.'

'OK, *Mr Sharman*, what can I do for you?'

'Cocaine,' I said.

'Yeah, man?'

227

'What's the score?'

He looked at Fiona. She looked him straight back in the eye. 'What? You buying or selling?'

'Neither, but say I was buying – is there any stuff about?'

'Round here? Get real, man, there's always stuff about.'

'I'm talking about good stuff. Maybe very good stuff, cheap and not full of Ajax and shit. Maybe a recent addition to the market place.'

'Could be.'

'Tell me more.'

'Why you want to know?'

'My business, man.'

'No, man, my business.'

'No, man, my fucking business,' I insisted.

'You been on the mother's little helper yourself, man?' he asked.

'I'll mother's little helper you, you cunt! I'm beginning to lose my patience. I'm wanted for murder, you know that? Two murders, three, who cares?' I pulled the Winchester from under my coat and rested its barrel on the edge of the table, pointing at his stomach. That way it didn't shake. 'If I pull this trigger, maaan, they'll be picking bits of you up three streets away. Now tell me the story and we'll remain friends, and you'll remain alive to party with those two babes tonight.'

'OK, man, cool,' he said, raising his hands in surrender. 'I got a good dealer. New money, up market. Not long on the scene. Primo gear.'

'What kind of place are they dealing from?'

'A house.'

'Security?'

'Nish on the premises, but I hear they got some heavy friends.'

'Amateurs,' I said.

'But getting rich at it.'

'If they screw with me, they're fucking rich history. Where?'

'Just around the corner.'

'Handy.'

'We were going round there after we quenched our thirst, the girls and me.'

'We'll tag along.'

'Not a good idea, man.'

'Yeah, man,' I said. 'A real good idea.' I tapped the shotgun on the wooden top. 'Think about it.'

'You could get me into serious trouble.'

'You're in that already, Malteser old buddy,' I said. 'And this is your chance to extricate yourself.' I finished my drink and got up.

'You mind if I make a call before we go?' he asked.

I wondered if he was pulling my leg. 'Sure,' I said, and got up and grabbed the telephone and pulled it hard. It stuck and I pulled again. It came away with a screech and a cloud of plaster and screws and Rawlplugs and a tangle of wires which I yanked out of the wall. I tossed it in his lap. 'There you go.'

The old dear who'd served me came running round to see what was happening. 'I'll have the police on you,' she shouted.

I grabbed Malteser and dragged him out into the street. 'Lead on, man,' I said. 'And be sensible.'

We walked back to the Sierra. It wasn't far.

Fiona drove, I sat in the back with Malteser who smoked nervously.

'What you want these people for? You going to turn them over?'

'We're going to turn someone over,' I said. 'Be sure you're not around when we do.'

He sat back in silence and smoked some more.

The dealer's house was on the Brixton/ Stockwell border, opposite a council estate. It was big, set slightly back off the road, three storeys, with a garage attached. A burglar alarm was mounted high and prominent above a first-floor window, with a blue light that would flash if the klaxon went off. A satellite dish was fixed to the front wall.

We cruised slowly by. There was a maroon Mercedes with full skirt option and maroon mags parked opposite, nose to nose with an AC Cobra. In front of the garage doors was a new BMW 7-series. Hardly council estate wheels. Unless there was a crack factory in the caretaker's apartment.

'Park round the corner,' I said to Fiona. 'Out of sight.'

She inched the Sierra round into a narrow street and parked.

I left Malteser in the back seat and got out of the car to talk to Fiona. 'I'm going in with him,' I said. 'You stay here.'

'I'm coming too.'

'No,' I said back. 'One of two things is going to happen. Either, it's a wipe and I'll be back in five minutes. Or it's a goer and someone will be along to collect me and take me to whoever's behind all this. If it's one, no problem. If it's two, follow us, then when we're wherever we're going, ring this number and speak to this guy.' I'd already written Endesleigh's name and office telephone number on a piece of paper. 'If he's not there, tell whoever is that it's a matter of life or death you get hold of him. Tell them it's about me, that should give you some clout. I am wanted for murder after all. When you get Endesleigh, and no one else will do, tell him what's up, and where I am, and that I'm in dire need of cavalry, quick. Got it?'

She nodded, but she wasn't happy. I didn't mention the third alternative, that I might get dead, real quick. But at least she'd be around to blow the whistle and see that I got a decent burial. 'Nick, I'd rather come with you,' she said. I think that was the first time she'd ever used my Christian name and I was touched.

'There's no one I'd rather have with me, you know that, but I need you out here. Park the car where you can see the house but they can't see you, and stay awake.'

'I will, darling.'

'I know.' And I kissed her.

'Be careful,' she said. 'I love you.'

I kissed her again and hauled Malteser out of the car, kicking the snow from the gutter off my boots. 'Let's do it,' I said to him.

We walked back round the corner. I held the scatter gun close to my body. We climbed the five white stone steps outside the front door and Malteser pushed the entry-phone button. A voice, it could have been male, female or anything in between, said something I didn't catch.

'Malteser,' he said, and the lock buzzed and we

pushed our way in. Bad mistake number one for the home team.

We stood in the hallway and I heard footsteps coming down from above. I looked up and the most beautiful woman I had ever seen, bar absolutely none, came clattering into sight on high, patent leather heels. She had so much black hair that I wondered how she kept her head erect against the weight. It billowed over her shoulders and down nearly to her waist. Her skin was as white as her hair was black and she showed plenty of it. Her black mini dress was cut low front and back. Her legs were bare.

'Malteser,' she said. She had a lovely voice, very posh.

'Amanda,' said Malteser. She kissed air two inches from each of his cheeks and held him back and looked at him.

'My dear,' she said. 'I'm so pleased to see you.'

It was sickening.

'Who's your friend?' asked Amanda, looking at me as if I were a zit that had appeared on her perfect skin overnight.

'A friend,' said Malteser.

'Is he all right?'

He looked at me, standing there with three days' growth of beard, dirty fingernails, speeded up to the eyeballs, dressed in a stupid hat and a filthy mac with a 12 gauge Winchester pump hidden beneath it, and said: 'Of course.'

'Just a regular junkie,' I said.

'You smell of drink,' she said dismissively, and dismissed me.

'Pardon me, I'm sure,' I said.

232

I noticed Malteser hadn't introduced us. No grasp of social niceties, see. 'Is Alistair about?' he asked.

Alistair! Jesus, I thought.

'Upstairs with the gang,' replied Amanda.

'Not the Purple Gang, I hope?' I said, bringing myself back into the conversation.

'I'm sorry, I don't understand,' she said. She was fucking polite, I'll say that for her, and fucking stupid for not searching me.

Bad mistake number two.

'Can I see him?' asked Malteser, as if God was upstairs doling out blow to the faithful.

'Of course, Malteser, you're always welcome.'

I thought maybe she was having a go at me.

She turned and started up the stairs and we followed her. I could hear music. It got louder, the higher we climbed. At the top of the stairs was a vestibule panelled in light wood. Amanda threw open a set of double doors. The room beyond was so big and bright it almost dazzled me. Most of the top floor had been knocked into one massive room. There must have been half an acre of polished parquet between us and the three sets of bay windows which allowed the cold winter light to flood in. There were no curtains at them, just venetian blinds pulled up to the pelmets.

Bad mistake number three.

The walls were painted white and had been left bare except for one canvas on the pristine plaster. The painting was by Picasso, from his Blue Period. The colours seemed to dance in front and behind my eyes. I wondered if it was an original or a copy. It must be a copy, I thought. No one in their right mind would hang an original Picasso in Brixton.

Hanging from the ceiling in the middle of the room was the biggest chandelier I've ever seen. The ceiling in the room was high but the chandelier dominated the room, and even in the harsh light of day it was lit. The crystal was a blaze of light that penetrated right through to the back of my skull like an electric shock.

Beyond the bare floor was a leisure area, thickly carpeted in blue to match the Picasso. Two huge sofas faced each other across a low Louis Quatorze table big enough and polished enough to play ice hockey on. A huge fireplace dominated the area. Logs burnt with an artificiality that had to be real. The room was stifling.

There were a couple of geezers in nice suits sitting on one of the sofas.

The CD player was churning out Nick Cave and the Bad Seeds at volume big. Next to it was a massive Panasonic monitor-style TV set wired up to a VCR and the satellite decoder. It must have had a fifty-inch screen, minimum. They're never much cop, big screen TVs. Lack of definition. And in the daylight and electric glare from the chandelier the picture was almost too faint to see. I could just make out it was showing a blue movie.

Next to the TV was a drinks trolley groaning with booze. On top of the polished table were two portable telephones lying so close together they could have been mating. Watching over them like a voyeur was a regular telephone plugged into the wall. A blond cat was sitting crosslegged in front of the table making lines from a pile of coke on an antique mirror two feet square. He was using a pearl-handled cut throat razor. A fifteen-foot high Christmas tree stood in one corner. It was bare except for one silver ball about twelve inches in diameter that hung and spun from one spikey green branch.

The blond cat stood up as Amanda, Malteser and I entered. He hit a button on the stereo remote and downed the volume to bearable.

I could hear the soundtrack to the movie then, if you could call sub *Pink Floyd* played in-store muzak style, and some fucker having his cock sucked with much smacking of lips, a soundtrack.

'Malteser,' the blond cat said, 'long time no see. It must be all of two days. That naughty nose will be the death of you yet.' He had a lovely voice too, perfect diction, just like Amanda. I was sure the pair of them would have been better off in Knightsbridge, rather than Brixton.

'Alistair,' said Malteser, 'can we talk?'

'Help yourself.'

'Privately,' I said.

Alistair looked at me and made the best value judgement so far. 'I think not,' he said.

'I need some coke,' said Malteser nervously.

'Doesn't everyone?'

'Yes,' said Malteser. 'No.' He looked over at me in desperation. 'It's difficult you see.'

'Same as always,' said Alistair. 'You give me money, I give you drugs. Simple. We've done it dozens of times before.'

'This time it's not going to be like before,' I said. Everyone in the room looked at me. All of a sudden I felt about as welcome as Joe Stalin at a Tory ladies' finger buffet.

'Who the fuck is this?' asked Alistair, and he looked at his two buddies on the sofa and grinned the sort of grin that said, 'Stick around, boys, we're going to have some fun here.' It was going to be a pleasure to rain all over his parade.

'He's pissed,' said Amanda. 'Why did you bring him here, Malteser?'

To huff and to puff and to blow your house down, I thought.

'He made me,' said Malteser, and his voice quivered.

'However did he do that?' asked Alistair, and I think his grin slipped just a fraction.

'Force of personality,' I said. 'Don't knock it.'

'So tell me – I'm sorry, I didn't catch your name . . .' I didn't enlighten him. 'Well, never mind,' he went on. 'How, pray, is it going to be different this time.' And he flicked the blade of the razor in and out of the handle and let it catch the light from the chandelier.

'This time we don't want *some* coke, we want *all* the coke,' I said.

'You jest,' he said, and that did it. I mean – 'You jest'. What did he think I was? A jumped up little wanker like him? I flicked back the skirt of my coat and brought the Winchester into the game.

'No,' I said, pointing it at his chest, 'I'm deadly serious. Now drop the razor and show me the volume merchandise.'

No one in the room so much as breathed and Alistair's grin vanished completely. He just stood and stared at the gun.

'The razor,' I said. He dropped it. 'Kick it over here.' He did as he was told. I stooped and picked it up, and tossed it on the empty sofa where it slipped between two cushions. I kept the scatter gun pointed straight at him all the while. 'The volume merchandise,' I reminded him.

'This is it,' said Alistair, pointing at the little pile on the mirror. His voice trembled.

'Bollocks!' I said. 'Pull the other one. It's holiday time and you're holding. I want to see it, and I'm not going until I have.'

'No,' said Amanda.

I moved the Winchester's barrel around the room, looking for a target. It passed across the Picasso and Alistair flinched. Christ, I thought, it *is* real. I moved the barrel back and worked the action.

'No!' he said.

'Yes,' I said back. 'Unless you cough the dope.'

'No,' said Amanda again. She was a cool one, but good sense prevailed.

'OK,' said Alistair, 'you win.' He went over to the Picasso. It was hinged on one side. He pulled the picture away from the wall to reveal a small combination safe. He put his hand up to the dial.

'Hold it,' I said. 'Does Amanda know the combination.'

'Yes.'

Bad mistake number four.

'Let her open it. And no silly games, Amanda.'

She went over and fiddled the dial back and forth and pulled a handle. The safe opened. She looked over at me and her eyes flashed green like a cat's. I pushed her aside. Inside, on the bottom shelf were three quarter-kilo bags of white powder. I pulled them out and examined them.

Bingo, I thought, and careless. One still had the remains of an HM Customs confiscation sticker on its side.

Amanda had taken the right hump. 'I'll get you for this, you black bastard!' she said to Malteser.

'Nice language,' I said. 'And from such a pretty mouth too.'

She spat at me and missed. I laughed in her face.

'Where did you get this stuff?' I asked.

'From a guy,' said Alistair.

'What guy?'

'I can't tell you that.'

'Yes, you can. You can tell me hard or easy, but believe me, in the end, you can.'

'I can't, they'll kill me.'

I laughed mirthlessly. 'And I suppose I can't?'

'Look, this is crazy. Can't we come to some kind of an arrangement?' pleaded Alistair.

'We are,' I said. 'You're going to tell me who your supplier is, and I'm going to leave you in peace to enjoy the festivities.'

'I can't do that. Look, there's money in the safe, lots, cash. Take that and the coke and go. I promise I won't tell anyone.'

'Alistair,' I said, 'you don't seem to be grasping exactly what I'm getting at here. Amazing as it may seem to you, I don't want your drugs or your money. I want to talk to whoever supplied you with this particular consignment.' I tapped the bag with the sticker. 'And nothing you can say or do will make me leave until I have. It's a nightmare come true, I admit, but there we are.'

'You can have anything I own except that,' he said desperately, and his eyes darted around the room. 'The picture,' he said. 'It's genuine, it's worth a fortune.'

I was getting tired, and I must admit, a trifle tetchy. I walked across the wooden floor and stuck the Winchester into Alistair's throat. I lifted the barrel under his chin until he came up on tiptoe. 'If I *wanted* the picture, or the money, or the drugs, I'd take them, but I don't. There's only *one* thing I do want. Now give it to me before I lose my temper.'

He tried one last desperate gambit. He looked over at Amanda. 'Take her,' he said, his voice a croak. 'She's good, she'll do anything you want.'

About then I started getting really pissed off at him. 'You're a piece of work, you know that, Alistair? You're in the wrong line. You should be a pimp. I'm sorry. No offence to your girlfriend, but I don't want her either.'

By this time the guy was trembling and sweating so much I thought he might have a seizure. 'Alistair,' I said, 'I'll tell you what. Give him a call. Tell him there's a guy here giving you a hard time. He'll come, I'll guarantee.'

Alistair thought about it.

'What about me?' asked Malteser.

I threw him one of the packets of coke, one without the sticker. 'You're not going to be too popular round here for a bit, Malt,' I said. 'You'd better take this and split. And, Malt—'

'Yeah?'

I put my finger to my lips but said nothing. He understood. He took the dope, turned and ran down the stairs. I heard the front door slam.

'Well, Alistair?' I said. And I pushed the barrel of the Winchester into his Adam's apple again.

He caved in then and said in a strangulated voice, 'All right, I'll do it. His name's Christian, that's all I know.'

'Call him,' I said gently, and pulled the barrel of the gun back. In a much softer tone I said, 'He'll understand.'

That seemed to calm Alistair down a bit. He picked up the telephone receiver and punched out a number. It was an 0836 number, so we were calling a portable. I guessed Alistair was past playing tricks, but I made him hold the telephone so that I could hear the ringing tone.

It was answered after two or three rings. 'Yes,' someone said tinnily.

I gestured for Alistair to answer. 'Christian,' he said, 'Alistair – I've got a problem.'

He paused.

'A nutter with a gun. He wants to see you.'

He listened.

'He says he wants to see our supplier.'

He listened again.

'Christ, I don't know! Why don't you speak to him yourself?'

I took the phone. 'Christian,' I said.

'Who's that?' Another strange voice.

'Nick Sharman. Get over here, pal. You and me gotta talk.'

Christian hung up.

25

Christian must have been out a-roving, because it was no more than ten minutes by my watch before the telephone rang. Whilst we'd been waiting I'd been attempting to keep everyone's spirits up. Alistair and Amanda weren't taking it too badly. The die had been cast, and being the fatalists they obviously were, they were prepared to let it fall as it would.

The guys on the sofa were a different matter. There they were, a pair of innocents with too much disposable income, who had just popped in for their Christmas supply of A-1 blow to impress the secretaries at the office Christmas party, or whatever. As a bonus they thought they might see some scruffy git get his face striped by their drug dealer, which would make an amusing story down at the local wine bar, and here they were embroiled in a world of violence and being held hostage at the point of a snub-nosed shotgun by a madman.

I made a few light-hearted comments about the weather and the price of fish but they didn't seem to go down too well, so I just watched them shifting about nervously in front of me, and smoked a couple of cigarettes. When the phone fluted, Alistair jumped and almost dropped the receiver as he picked it up. 'Careful,' I warned. 'Let's not say anything that could be misconstrued.'

He gulped and said, 'Yes?' into the phone. He listened for a few moments, then held the receiver away from his face and said to me, 'He wants you to give me your gun, and then I'm to search you.'

'I'm not handing over a loaded gun,' I said. 'I think Amanda might use it on me. I'm not going to shoot him. He knows what I want.'

Alistair passed on the message, listened again and came back to me. 'He won't come up until he sees me at the window holding it.'

'And the rest of Stockwell too,' I said, and grimaced and worked the action. I pumped all five cartridges through the Winchester. They rattled on to the carpet. I picked them up and lined them up on the table in front of me like a row of red-coated soldiers again. I unhooked the scatter gun from its harness and tossed it to Alistair. He fumbled the catch and put it on the table. 'Now I've got to search you.'

I stood up and took off the dirty trench coat and threw it on the sofa. I raised my arms. 'Go ahead,' I said. 'But, remember, I'm ticklish.'

I stood there in leather jacket and jeans and Alistair searched me thoroughly. Then he picked up the coat and patted it down.

'Satisfied?' I asked when he was finished. He nodded and went back to the phone. 'He's clean,' he said, then put down the receiver and picked up the Winchester and went to the window, holding the gun up in front of him.

Alistair came back from the window. He put the

gun back on the table, picked up the telephone, listened for a second, nodded, but said nothing and replaced it on the hook. 'He's on his way up.'

A few seconds later the entry-phone buzzer sounded and Alistair answered. He pressed the button to open the front door and we all waited. I heard footsteps on the stairs, and then a voice.

'Sharman, show yourself at the door, arms above your head.' I did as I was told. The staircase itself was dark, but I stood in the light coming from the room. 'Turn around,' the voice ordered. Once again I did as I was told. I heard the sound of the bolt of an automatic weapon being thrown and footsteps again and felt cold metal on my neck. 'Cocked and ready, son,' whispered the voice. 'Walk into the room, and no messing.' Again I obeyed. 'OK, turn around.' I did, and saw a good-looking black guy in a tweed overcoat open over a dark jacket and grey trousers, a white button down shirt, neat tie and black shoes. He looked like a schoolteacher except for the S&W 9mm semi-automatic he held comfortably in his right hand.

'Nice touch, the gun,' I said. 'It takes all the formality out of the rest of the outfit.'

'Shut up,' said the black man wearily.

'Aren't you going to introduce us, Alistair?' I said. 'I'm Nick Sharman. You must be Christian.' I put out my hand.

Christian just stood there. 'Don't screw around,' he said. 'Let's go.' So we went.

He wrapped the shotgun in my mac and tucked it under his arm and put the shells into the side pocket of his coat which spoiled the line somewhat, but I said not a word. He allowed the folds of the mac to cover his gun hand too. 'Just walk to the car,' he said. 'No tricks.'

'No tricks,' I said. It wasn't him I wanted to see anyway.

When we got to the street I couldn't see the Sierra. I didn't look too hard, I didn't want Christian getting suspicious. But I thought that it would be just my luck if Fiona had suddenly been taken short and was right then racing round looking for a ladies' loo.

Christian gestured at a gun-metal grey Audi parked a few car lengths down the road. A tiny red light behind the windscreen showed that it was alarmed up. 'That's us,' he said.

He took a remote control from his coat pocket with his left hand and pressed a button. The red light winked out. I walked in front of him to the car. 'Doors are open,' he said. I got in the passenger side, he got behind the wheel and shoved the shotgun on to the back seat. 'I don't really need this, do I?' he said, referring to the pistol.

'No,' I replied.

'You couldn't take it off me anyway,' he said. 'I'd beat your shit in.' And the gun disappeared under his coat.

Thus warned, I put on my seat belt and waited for the magical mystery tour.

Before he switched on the engine, he picked up the phone, punched out a number and said: 'Got him.'

He drove the car out of Stockwell, through Clapham to Battersea. I didn't look back once, but I wanted to.

I wondered if we were going to the lock-up, but

we went past, down Silverthorne Road, into some back doubles and out in Queenstown Road opposite a block of nouveau desirable shops and restaurants. He pointed at one restaurant in particular, with a frontage twice as long as any of the others and a sign that read LET THE GOOD TIMES ROLL in dead neon over the front. Outside was parked a familiar looking BMW with a large figure in the driver's seat. 'That's it,' he said.

'Smart place,' I said. 'Em did do well. Smart name too.'

'But I don't think they're going to roll for you,' said Christian.

'You'd be surprised,' I replied. 'I can be the life and soul of any party.'

'Not this one,' he said dryly, spotted a gap in the traffic and pulled into the side road at the end of the block, then into an alley at the back where he stopped behind Teddy's Suzuki.

A full set, I thought.

'Out you get.'

I did as I was told, and he fetched the Winchester and propelled me through a door set in a high fence, across a yard and through another door into the kitchen of the restaurant. The kitchen was empty and cold, and haunted with the spicy ghosts of old cooking.

'Let the staff off early?' I asked.

'We're closed.'

'And at the busiest time of the year too. Emerald won't be pleased.'

'He's in no position to do anything about it.'

But he will, pal, eventually, I thought.

Christian closed and locked the kitchen door

behind us, left the key in the lock, and walked me
through the large dining room which was dim and
shadowy but looked comfortable and expensive,
with a huge bar along one wall, well stocked with
spirits and mixers and all the paraphernalia of the
cocktail barman's trade. At the back of the bar
was a mirror, fully twenty foot long, and I saw my
reflection, which was none too clever.

He showed me another door in the side wall of
the room, marked 'Staff Only', which opened on
to a flight of bare stairs leading upwards. I walked
up in front of him, through another door, and down
a corridor. He stopped me outside a door about
half way down, marked 'Private'. He rapped on
the frame with his fist.

'Come in,' said a voice I half recognised, and
Christian gestured for me to open the door, which I
did.

26

It was a tiny office, with just one barred window that allowed a little of the afternoon light to creep in over the sill before it was suffocated by the pall of cigarette and cigar smoke that floated across the room at shoulder height. The real illumination came from three low wattage fixtures set into the polystyrene ceiling. They gave off a custard yellow light that seemed to add to the gloom rather than dispel it. The room looked as if it had been furnished from the remnants of a garage sale, with a scarred wooden desk, clear except for a telephone and a huge ashtray overflowing with butts and ash, three chairs and a two-seater sofa that had seen better days. The walls were nicotine-coloured and the carpet was a dirty green that had been worn scabby in front of the desk and at the door.

The room was too crowded with people for comfort. Lupus sat in the Capo's chair behind the desk, sucking on a Havana. Jack Dark sat primly on an upright armchair in front of the desk, Ronnie's bulk about filled the sofa and Teddy stood leaning against the wall by the window, smoking a cigarette. The room smelt of sweat and deceit and stale smoke.

Christian pushed me inside, but not hard enough for me to retaliate. The four men already in the room looked at me, and I looked right back. 'Hail, hail, the gang's all here,' I said. But they weren't.

Christian threw the shotgun on to the desk and scattered the shells around it. 'Heavy artillery,' he said. 'Not friendly.'

'Sharman,' said Lupus, ignoring the gun, 'we've been expecting you.'

'Really?' I said. 'Did you bake a cake?'

'Get on with it,' said Jack Dark. 'We're not here for conversation.'

'What are we here for then?' I asked.

'As if you didn't know,' said Dark.

'I'm here to help Emerald, like I always was,' I said.

'And yourself,' said Dark.

These people had no concept of friendship. To them, friends were people you used, or who used you.

'No,' I said, 'just Emerald.'

'Bullshit!' said Lupus. 'People like you don't give a shit for people like us. You smelt money, big money. We tried to kill you off and that didn't work. Then Dark sticks his nose in and tried to buy you off. Stupid bastard!' He gave Dark a particularly nasty stare. 'You just kept coming. Now you're here for the big pay-off.'

'Wrong,' I said. 'I've been looking for who framed him. I don't want any part of the money.'

'Then you're more of a mug than I thought.' Teddy spoke for the first time.

'Teddy,' I said, 'it really is you. I thought some-one had pissed against the wall.'

His face suffused with blood and his nostrils flared. He came off the wall, fists clenched.

'Stay still,' said Lupus.

'That's right,' I agreed. 'Stay still. If you come near me, I'll break your bloody neck.'

'Big talk,' he sneered.

'I'd believe him, if I were you,' said Lupus calmly. 'He's capable of doing it.'

Teddy subsided against the wall again, but kept screwing me, as if maybe I'd wilt like a flower out of water. Fat chance.

The telephone on the desk rang suddenly. Lupus scooped up the receiver and listened without speaking. He put it down after ten seconds or so. Everyone looked at him, but he said nothing.

'How *did* you find us?' asked Jack Dark after a moment.

'I was lucky. I found one of your customers and they co-operated.' Lupus gave Christian a killing look. 'Don't worry,' I said, 'I would have kept on stirring the shit until the turd I was looking for popped up. You just made it a little easier. It was very careless of you to leave a bit of a customs sticker on the packet.' Another killer look passed from Lupus to Christian. They were flying around all over the place this afternoon. 'You're not the pros I took you for. And as for those two who were fronting for you – Jesus, they were a bust waiting to happen.'

'They had the right connections,' said Dark. 'And there's plenty more where they came from.'

'Sure,' I said. 'Everyone's dispensable, even your supplier. And with him dead, I guess the game was about over. Were you doing business with him long?'

'Long enough,' said Lupus.

'But why did you kill him?'

'He got chicken,' said Dark. 'And greedy. He liked the money but he was afraid of getting pulled.'

'Who can blame him?' I asked. 'Most people are.'

'If you can't do the time . . .' said Dark. 'He knew what he was letting himself in for. Then he got a conscience and decided we'd be better off out of the way.'

'You didn't have to torture them.'

'He asked for it,' said Dark. 'Nobody crosses me.' He said it with such certainty that I believed him.

'And the woman too?'

'What was I supposed to do? He wouldn't talk, the crazy bastard. He took my money, screwed me on the deal, tried to turn us in and when that didn't work, fucked off, vanished. I don't know who he thought he was dealing with. It was a bit of a surprise when we turned up on his doorstep. And he still wouldn't tell me where the cash was. So Ronnie here had to show him the error of his ways.' Ronnie almost blushed. 'But it wasn't until we started on that tart he was shacking up with that he'd tell us where he'd put the money.'

'How did you find him?'

'The woman. She was straight. Had a kid, a little boy who lived with her mother. She had to take his Christmas presents round. Stupid slag. We had someone watching the mother's flat, and he fol-

lowed her to where they were hiding out. We
heard about it as we were leaving the Indian, so
we made a detour.'

'How the hell did he know to call me?'

'You've got a friend on the force, haven't you?'
said Dark.

'Yes.'

'When he started sniffing around, Taylor got to
hear about you.'

Taylor had sent out a cry for help, and I hadn't
answered. Nice one, Nick!

I could still smell the stench in the flat and see
the faces of the man and woman who'd died in
agony. It was another little debt I had to pay back.

'And when I did go, I took one of yours with me.' I
looked at Teddy who was still screwing me. 'You
must have thought it was your birthday.'

'We did,' said Dark. 'But it was lucky for you
you called him and he called us. If you'd turned up
while we were there, we'd've done for you too.
Especially after that malarky with Ronnie in the
restaurant. It just seemed like a better idea to
leave you around for the coppers to find.' He
looked over at Teddy. 'If he'd have hit you a bit
harder, you'd be out of our hair now.'

'Banged up with Emerald in jail, you mean?'

'Right.'

'It's just as well I've got a hard head, then. So
Emerald was telling me the truth all along. He
really doesn't know anything about all this.'

'That's right,' said Lupus. 'We just used him for
what we needed. He's getting old and stupid and
soft. When he bought his bloody restaurant, he
thought he could just sit back and enjoy life.'

'Such loyalty,' I said. 'Weren't you making enough money on the straight?'

'There's never enough money,' said Teddy.

'You're the worst of the lot,' I said with as much contempt in my voice as I could muster. 'You're his own flesh and blood. I thought he was looking after you.'

He didn't even bother to grace the remark with an answer.

'So if Emerald had nothing to do with the drug dealing, why did Taylor grass him?' I asked.

'He didn't,' said Lupus, and smiled mirthlessly. 'He grassed an address. It was the old man's hard luck that his name was on the lease. Taylor thought Teddy owned the lock-up. Some joke! He doesn't even own the suit he's wearing. Watkins, see, but Old Bill nicked the wrong Watkins and it worked out good for us.'

'But not for Em.'

He nodded.

'How did you find Taylor in the first place?'

'Same old story. He needed money. He had a house he couldn't afford down near the coast. A car he couldn't afford. A wife he couldn't afford, and he liked women and gambling. Expensive women, and he was a lousy gambler. Teddy used to see him around the clubs. He likes gambling too. One time Taylor was drunk and coked up and on a losing streak, not that that was unusual. He told Teddy he could get as much stuff as he wanted, at a good price and in bulk. It's not surprising considering half the dope confiscated in England ended up with him. My old friend there, Jack, put up the cash and we used a few of the boys who were fed up with going straight to help us out. They were glad to do it. There's not a lot of excitement in catering these days.'

'But why did you leave the stuff lying about when you'd been tipped off that the law was going to bust the lock-up?' I asked.

'We didn't,' said Lupus. 'We went down and cleared the place out, at what, ten that night? Taylor planted the stuff later. He didn't even know that we knew anything was up. We certainly weren't going to hang around and watch what happened, were we?'

'But half a million quid's worth!' I said. 'Wasn't it a bit excessive?'

'He wanted to make sure everyone involved went down hard,' said Dark. 'No bail or anything. He didn't care what he did. He was getting flakey. His bosses knew he was up to something. He was spending dough like water. He got the shits and done a runner. He didn't want to be caught with any gear on him, so he dumped it on us. He already had the cash. If he hadn't panicked, none of this would have happened. Thank Christ he didn't know I was bank-rolling the deal.'

'But didn't the law suspect you lot?' I said to Lupus. 'After all, you were working for Emerald.'

'Course,' he said. 'Everybody's been pulled up this week, even the bloody waiters downstairs. But we're all clean as the driven. Even the old man doesn't suspect us. His own flesh and blood, and me, a lawyer with a pristine record. As far as he's concerned we're all being fitted up. And until they can prove different, as far as the law's concerned, his name was on the lease and his name was on the warrant. All we needed to do was sell the last of what we had, then sit back and enjoy the proceeds.'

'While Emerald takes the fall.'

'Ironic, isn't it?' asked Lupus. 'And it would all have worked out but for you.'

'I'm flattered,' I said, but not so flattered that they were taking time to tell me everything. I knew that there was only one reason, and that was that they didn't plan for me to leave, not vertically anyway.

'Don't be,' said Lupus. 'And don't think your girlfriend is dropping ten pence to the local police station either. Because she's not.'

He saw the look on my face and laughed. 'Give us some credit,' he said. 'We didn't come over on the last banana boat, even if some of us look like we did.'

As if on cue, the door behind me opened. I looked round and my old pal, who I'd last seen sitting in the jump seat of Emerald's stretch Lincoln, came in pushing Fiona in front of him.

She looked as cranky as hell, mad at him and herself. If we hadn't been in such a mess it would have been almost funny. She was giving him severe GBH of the ear drums as she came in.

'Don't push me, you git,' she said as he propelled her through the door.

'Get inside and shut up,' said Jump Seat. Then to Lupus: 'This bitch is pure poison, boss. Why don't we shut her up for good?'

'Later, Eddie,' said Lupus. 'Can't you control the girl? A big man like you.'

Eddie pushed Fiona to the empty chair and

forced her to sit. I made half a move in his direction and Christian showed me his gun and shook his head. 'Tough guys,' I said, keeping the contempt in my voice.

'Shut up, Sharman,' said Ronnie. 'You're full of shit.'

'Blimey!' said Fiona. 'A talking pig. You should join the circus, mate. You'd make a fortune.'

'He's already in one,' I said.

'Shut up, both of you,' said Dark. 'Or Ronnie'll shut you up.'

'Bollocks,' said Fiona. 'How do you expect me to take you seriously, wearing a syrup like that?'

Dark's face reddened. She'd obviously hit a soft spot.

'If she speaks again, gag her,' said Lupus.

'Don't waste your breath on them,' I said to her. She looked at me and I winked. I knew I had to do something or we were both dead, and hoped she got the meaning of my wink.

Christian's gun hand had relaxed when he realised I wasn't going to go for Eddie, and I saw that he had moved further into the room. As everyone else seemed to be looking at Fiona, I moved slightly back towards the door. Not enough to be noticed, I hoped, except by her. She did. 'If any of you cunts try to gag me, I'll bite your fucking hands off,' she snarled.

'Do it,' said Lupus, and Eddie shoved between me and Christian to get to her. Fiona kicked Christian hard on the shin and he cried out in surprise. I caught hold of Eddie and pushed him hard into Christian who was almost hopping in pain. Eddie tripped and stumbled against him and they both nearly fell. I turned and found the door handle and tugged the door open, ran into the corridor and slammed the door behind me.

It was the only chance we had, for me to leave her behind. I didn't want to do it, but what choice did I have? It was a decision I was going to regret bitterly.

27

The corridor stretched in both directions, swing
doors at either end. I turned right, in the opposite
direction from which Christian had brought me. It
would be logical for me to go back the way we'd
come, or at least I hoped he'd think that. I ran
towards the door and my leg started acting up
again. I did the last two steps in an awkward half
jump and hit the door hard. It flew open. Behind me
I heard crashing and shouting from the office.

The door led to a store room. It was at least thirty
feet high, dark, cold, and concrete-floored. Every
flat surface was stacked with boxes and cartons
and crates of spirits and beer. The only escape was
a door out to the back, leading God knew where. I
slammed it open. Pitch dark, with just the impression of stairs leading downwards. Beside the door
was a flight of metal steps leading upwards to a
shadowy gallery that ran around three walls of the
room which was also piled with boxes and crates.
I bounced on my DMs and went up. I was tired of
being chased. I figured any pursuers would go
through the door and downstairs, especially as the
door was still swinging gently on its hinges. Then I
could sneak back and try and get to Fiona.

I went as far round the gallery as I could and

crouched down deep in the shadows and waited. From where I was I could see both doors and the bottom of the steps. I didn't have to wait more than a few seconds before Christian pushed slowly through the door from the corridor, gun in hand. He was alone. My hackles rose as I saw him.

He flattened himself against the wall, swept the room with the gun and walked across the floor. He kicked open the door to the stairs, peered through, then turned and looked up. I thought he must see me and scrunched down even further. Christian moved towards the steps. If I'd had a gun I could have shot him in the back. I pushed myself as far into the shadows as I could and my arm touched a litre bottle of lemonade which was standing on the balcony.

I saw it start to topple and grabbed for it. My fingers brushed the smooth glass but only managed to push it harder. It wobbled and fell and as it went it touched its twin standing next to it. They both rolled across the metal and over the edge of the balcony. Christian was just putting his foot on the bottom step. He heard the sound, stopped and turned. His gun swung round with him, and then up in my direction. He thought he was in no danger, that he might just get his pant cuffs wet, and even took time to watch as the bottles fell. He didn't even flinch. The two bottles hit the concrete floor simultaneously and burst like grenades. As they hit, he fired.

The first shot from the pistol hit the metal banister about a yard from my head. The second spanged off the floor. I ducked down, deafened by the shots and the sound of the bottles exploding. I

listened for his footsteps on the stairs but could
hear nothing for the ringing in my ears.

I peered out over the guard rail and saw him
walking around in an erratic circle with his hands
over his face. He seemed to be covered in blood.
There was blood leaking from behind the fingers
of his hand that was clutching at his eye. Even
through battered eardrums I could hear him
screaming. He seemed to be squeezing blood out of
his head like pus from a huge boil. The gun was on
the floor in a puddle of liquid. I ran around the
balcony and down the steps before he could pick it
up, but he wasn't interested. He was too busy tear-
ing at the neck of one of the bottles that had
embedded itself in his eye socket, twist off cap
outward. He fell to his knees and then face down
on the floor and twitched and screamed until I
smacked him on the head a couple of times with the
barrel of the pistol and he was quiet. He smelt like
something you add to a drop of gin.

The gun was sticky with blood and lemonade. I
wiped it and my hands on the legs of my jeans. I
pushed the door to the corridor just wide enough to
attach one eye to the gap. Nothing stirred. I started
to giggle with nerves and bit down on my underlip
to contain them. I was shaking like a shitting dog.

No good, Sharman, I thought. You've had your
luck for the day. Now it's down to you.

I felt like going home.

I went to the door leading to the stairs, stepping
over Christian's still form as I went, then down and
through yet another swing door into the restaurant
proper. I stood in the doorway for a moment. The
dining room seemed deserted.

As I stepped in, Ronnie appeared from the kitchen holding a gun, and fired. The bullet ripped half a yard of wood from the door frame beside my head. I returned a shot and he ducked back. I ran across the room, snaking between the tables, and threw myself behind the bar. I looked over the top, and the door from the kitchen began to open slowly. I steadied my gun on the polished wood of the bar and waited. Ronnie's gun hand appeared, and then his head and shoulders. He looked quickly from side to side but didn't see me.

I squeezed off a shot. He shouted in pain, pushed the door wide and stood in the doorway, firing. Bottles and glasses exploded all around me and the mirror behind the bar shattered into a million pieces. The noise was deafening. The restaurant filled with smoke and stink from the guns. I aimed at his silhouette and fired twice. That's for Taylor and his girlfriend, I thought, as I pulled the trigger and the gun kicked in my hand. Ronnie fell back against the door jamb and slid down to a sitting position. His gun was silent.

I slid from behind the bar and went over to him. I pulled the gun from his hand and stuck it into the waistband of my jeans. I pushed open the kitchen door. It looked deserted but I couldn't hear shit from the ringing in my ears. There might have been a marching band in the pantry for all I would have known.

I held the kitchen door open and looked back into the restaurant, wondering what to do next. I didn't have to think for long. The door marked 'Staff Only' burst open and Eddie crashed through, carrying a revolver. I snapped off a shot and

missed. He returned fire and slid under a table.
The bullet clanged off something metallic behind
me. I ducked down and let the door swing shut.
Next to it was a closed serving hatch. I inched it
open and got a sliver of wood in my face from a
couple of bullets for my troubles. The serving hatch
door was blown open and slammed back against
the wall. I threw myself down, rolled under a
cutting table and pulled out the splinter. The sharp
end was pink. I lay still and listened. It seemed like
hours before I heard a sound from the restaurant. I
pulled myself in tighter and risked a peek. Nothing.

I wondered if Eddie would come through the
door or poke his head over the hatch. I guessed the
hatch and pointed my gun in that direction. Nothing again. Then I saw the top of a nappy head and a
gun-filled hand and a pair of eyes coming over the
edge of the hatch, and fired once. He fired back
three times and the table took a lot of damage.
Through numbed ears I heard the click of the
hammer on an empty cartridge case. I rolled out
and stood up and looked through the hatch. Eddie
was fumbling in his pocket for cartridges. The
cylinder of his gun was open.

I rested my gun hand against the cold metal and
tapped gently on the counter top. 'Knock, knock,' I
said.

He made as if to slam the cylinder shut. 'Don't
even think about it,' I said.

'Shit,' was all he said back. He dropped gun and
cartridges on to the floor.

'Come into my parlour,' I said.

He came to his feet and pushed through the door.
I kept my gun on him all the way. 'On the deck, face

down,' I ordered. 'Put your hands flat on the floor, arms extended.'

He looked at me as if he was going to spit. I knew how he felt. But he obliged. 'What happened to the girl?' I asked, when he was comfy.

'She's dead, motherfucker.'

Not again, I thought. Oh Jesus Christ almighty, not again. When someone you love dies it's like being blindfolded in a room without windows or lights at midnight. It's blacker than the inside of a closed grave. I grabbed a handful of his hair. It was short, but thick, and I got a good handful. I pulled his head up off the floor and screwed the end of my gun barrel in his ear. The hammer was back and I applied pressure on the trigger with a trembling finger. His eyes widened and he opened his mouth to speak again. Suddenly there was no more pressure and the gun fired and all that came out of his mouth was a gout of blood. The gun was so close to his skull that it kicked clean out of my hand and blood and brains blew all over the floor and his scalp went loose in my hand. I let go of his hair and his head hit the floor like an overripe melon. His body jerked convulsively and his bowels opened.

I picked up the gun and checked the load. There was one bullet in the breech and the clip was empty. Ronnie's magnum held two live cartridges. I ditched them both and took Eddie's .38 revolver. I loaded it, stuck the spare cartridges in my pocket and went looking for the others.

I went slowly up the stairs, through the swing door and along the corridor. All was quiet. I stood outside the office door. It stood slightly ajar. I could see that the lights inside were still on. I pushed the door open with my fingertips and stepped into the room. At first I thought it was empty. Then I noticed Fiona's boots poking out from behind the desk. I felt dizzy as I walked over and looked at her. She was lying face down on the carpet. I knelt and gently rolled her over. There was a lump the size of a golf ball on her forehead, a bruise up into her hairline and dried blood at the side of her mouth. I knelt and gently cradled her in my arms. I closed my eyes for a moment and when I opened them again she was looking at me.

'Is this love, Sharman?' she asked, and her voice cracked.

I was so surprised I nearly dropped her. 'He told me you were dead,' I said.

'Who did?'

'It doesn't matter.'

She smiled weakly. 'Mind you, it might be an improvement. My bloody head's killing me.'

'What happened?'

'I don't know. The last thing I remember is kicking that spade, and then the one who dragged me out of the phone box when I was going to phone that copper mate of yours, put my lights out.'

'He's dead. So's the one you kicked.'

'I didn't kick him to death, did I?' she asked, and using my shoulder and the edge of the desk dragged herself to her feet.

'No,' I said. 'You didn't. Are you going to be all right?'

'I'll survive.'

'I wonder why they didn't finish you off. It must be your lucky day.'

'Thanks, Sharman!'

'I'm going to call the police,' I said. I picked up the receiver of the telephone on the desk. It was dead. I followed the wire with my eyes. The junction box had been torn from the wall. 'Damn!' I said.

'What are we going to do?'

'Go after them. This isn't over yet.'

As we left the room, I realised that someone had taken the Winchester and the shells off the desk.

I turned left outside the office door and we went back down the corridor. On the landing at the top of the stairs was a fire door. It was open. I looked through and down into the alley at the back of the restaurant.

Teddy and Lupus and Dark were standing by the Suzuki. There was a Gladstone bag on the bonnet of the jeep and they seemed to be arguing about it – possession of it had obviously been more important than tying up loose ends, like Fiona. Teddy was holding the Winchester. 'When thieves fall out,' I said. 'Let's go down and see what all the fuss is about.'

We didn't use the fire escape. If Teddy had seen us we would have been sitting targets, like tin ducks in a shooting gallery. We went back down to the restaurant. I warned Fiona it wasn't pretty. It wasn't. The dining room and kitchen stank of smoke and shit. It was enough to put you off eating out for life. I turned the key of the lock in the kitchen door and opened it. We walked across the yard and I heard raised voices.

I opened the door into the alley just in time to see Teddy blow Jack Dark in half with the shotgun. Literally in half. Fiona's old man hadn't been kidding about the power of the load in the shells he'd given me. Most of Dark's smoking body flew across the bonnet of Christian's Audi, and the car alarm screamed. I saw Dark's wig flop into a puddle like a dead ginger rat. I fired through the door at Teddy and missed.

He turned the shotgun towards me and blew the door and half the fence to sawdust. As I saw the Winchester move, I threw myself back at Fiona and knocked her over. I landed on top of her and protected her with my body as we were covered with splinters of wood. I actually saw the muzzle flash as we fell, and heard the boom and the whistle of the shot.

We stayed down until I heard a car door slam, and the engine start. I got up, found my gun where it had fallen, and looked through the wreckage of the fence just in time to see the jeep pull away fast, and turn into the road at the end of the alley, out of my sight. I stuck the gun in the pocket of my leather jacket, grabbed Fiona's hand, and we ran after it.

28

As the jeep skidded into Queenstown Road we ran out of the alley in the same direction. When we reached the corner I saw Jack Dark's BMW parked in front of the entrance to the restaurant. Jim was in the driver's seat. I saw his head move round as he watched the Suzuki narrowly miss a black cab and accelerate away, heading south. He opened the driver's door and stepped carefully over the black muck at the kerbside. He was so busy saving his shiny shoes that he didn't see us.

I grabbed Fiona's hand and we ran towards him. He heard our footsteps on the pavement and looked up, his face registering, first surprise, then anger, or fear, or something combining both. He went to reach under his jacket. He didn't have a chance, we were too close.

I kept going, pivoted on my bad foot, which sent a lance of white hot pain up one side of my body, and kicked him hard between his legs with my right. He doubled up and spat out a scream which cut off when I brought my knee up into his face. I heard cartilage fracture and blood spurted from his broken nose. He fell against the door of the car, which creaked under his weight, and hit the pavement with a wet slap. I didn't check his health. He was out of the game, but I kicked him hard on the side of the head to make sure.

I shoved Fiona through the door and over the console to the passenger seat. I scrambled into the driver's side. The key was in the ignition. I tugged at the door but it caught on Jim's body and wouldn't close. I was almost gibbering with frustration as I tried to pull it over his dead weight. I stuck my good foot out of the car and shoved at him and he groaned and rolled away. I slammed the door and turned the key and the engine caught first time. I thanked God for the automatic box and snicked the gear stick into drive, spun the power assisted steering wheel, floored the accelerator, and the car surged away from the kerb and roared up the right hand side of the road. We overtook a bus and sped after Teddy and Lupus. The road curved just before climbing towards the lights at the junction with the Wandsworth Road and I saw the jeep turning left on the red in front of a long, double queue of motors.

I pulled into the oncoming traffic and switched the lights to full beam, put my left hand on the horn ring and held it there. Cars pulled over to the kerb to avoid us, their horns joining the cacophony. I hit the brake hard, spun the wheel and turned left into Wandsworth Road, whipping the car around the wrong side of the central reservation on two wheels. The back of the BMW slammed into the front nearside of a Mini-Metro and ripped off its bumper. The BMW rocked as if it was going to overturn. I corrected the skid by flooring the accelerator once more and letting the wheel spin back through my fingers. The offside wing just touched the side of a post office van.

The car righted itself and we were racing towards Vauxhall again. I registered the startled faces of drivers and pedestrians with black Os for mouths and Fiona shouted something I didn't hear. I was sweating and grinning and knew we'd catch them or rack up the big car in the attempt.

I bullied my way past another couple of cars, but the road was too narrow and lined with parked cars on both sides, the oncoming traffic too heavy for us to gain much on the jeep. The next set of lights was in our favour and I spotted the Suzuki maybe five or six cars ahead. Headlights were flashing behind me angrily but I ignored them. I pulled around two more cars and through another set of green lights before Teddy noticed anything. Suddenly the jeep accelerated through the traffic, dodging and weaving and setting off horns and flashing lights in its wake. He overtook a truck on the inside at the lights by the South Bank Poly. The jeep picked up speed as the road widened for the final run up to Vauxhall Cross.

I slapped the gear stick into low drive and almost stood on the kickdown. The BMW's rear end dropped and its bonnet rose. The engine screamed and I felt G-force push me back in my seat. I drove around the wrong side of a bollard and pulled level with the jeep. I spun the wheel hard left again and slammed into the side of the Suzuki with a rending of metal and a shower of sparks. The BMW weighed twice as much as the jeep. The smaller vehicle careered off and hit the kerb.

It bounced back. I saw Teddy's face through the driver's window, contorted with rage. Lupus stuck the shotgun through the side canvas.

'Down,' I shouted, and floored the brake pedal as he fired. Fiona hit the carpet and I ducked just as most of the nearside wing and the bonnet were blown off the BMW. It skidded in the wet and started to spin. I let her go and we skated around three times before I could control the skid. The tyres screeched as I corrected left, right, left, and we came to a halt, still pointing towards Vauxhall. I spun the rear wheels and took off again.

We got up to seventy as we passed Sainsbury's and caught up with the jeep. I rammed the back of it and lumps of metal flew off both cars. The BMW bounced over something heavy, and Lupus fired through the back of the soft top. It shredded, and I ducked, and the windscreen blew inwards and showered us with laminated glass. I slowed, stuck my head up into the slipstream and saw the jeep pull away into the traffic coming into Wandsworth Road to avoid the jam at the lights at the junction with Nine Elms Lane. I followed.

Steam started to fill the inside of the car. The power steering was gone, but I stuck behind the jeep as it busted through the railings and bounced across the central barrier and back into the stream of traffic. The lights at the bridge were green and we shot across the junction into Albert Embankment. I knew that the BMW was about done, and saw a blue flashing light up by the roundabout. Teddy must have seen it too because the jeep slowed and turned into Black Prince Road. I was right behind it. The road was crowded with parked cars on both sides.

Teddy slammed on the brakes and Lupus leaned

over the tailgate of the jeep and blew the front off-side wheel clean off the BMW. I skidded and hit the side of a parked van. We ended up slewed across the road under the railway bridge in another shower of sparks and the stink of burnt rubber. The engine stalled and I turned the key, but the BMW was dead. I jumped out of the car through the undamaged driver's door and watched as the Suzuki pulled away.

I slammed my fist on the roof of the car. Fiona tried to open the passenger door but it was jammed. She scrambled over the driver's seat and joined me in the street. 'Damn it,' I said.

Behind us I heard the sound of a truck horn and a skip lorry slowed to a halt with a hiss of hydraulics. A big Ford seventeen-tonner with IVECO TURBO in chrome letters across the front of the cab, almost hidden by a matt black, custom built bumper of tempered steel, bolted on to scare the civilians. Tucked behind the bumper at a rakish angle was a filthy teddy bear with one arm missing, wearing a faded blue waistcoat. The driver leaned out of his window and said, 'Get that shit out of my way.'

I grinned at Fiona and pulled the pistol that I'd taken from Eddie out of my pocket. 'No,' I said. 'You get your shit out of my way.'

He looked at me as if I was mad. 'What?'

'I said, get out of there. I want that truck.'

'Is this a fucking joke, or what?'

'It must be or what,' I said, and just to prove it, I shot the side window out of a Vauxhall Cavalier parked at the kerb, which burst inward in a most satisfying way. About then the little crowd that had gathered to see what all the excitement was about, decided that they all had urgent business elsewhere and dispersed back to their offices and warehouses with a good story to tell at their tea breaks.

'OK, mate,' the skip lorry driver said. 'I believe you. Take the fucking thing.'

'Out,' I said. 'And don't touch the keys.' He climbed out and left the engine running. I boosted Fiona up into the cab and followed her. I kept the gun on him and he backed away with his hands up in a placating gesture.

I got behind the big steering wheel and pushed down the clutch pedal which was heavy and stiff. My leg stabbed me again and I knew I was about done too. I ignored the pain, gritted my teeth and threw the gear stick into first. I tried to engage the clutch but my leg shook with the effort. We jumped forward and hit the BMW hard. The truck stalled.

'Fuck it!' I said, and put it into neutral.

I turned the key and the engine caught. I put it into reverse and did a better job at the second attempt. The truck moved slowly backwards. Clutch, first gear again . . . I was relieved to feel power in the steering and turned the wheel hard down to the right. The huge truck pushed the BMW out of the way with a screech of metal on metalled surface. We bumped up the kerb and down again and were off.

I found second with a crash of gears and put my foot down. The turbo assisted engine answered with a good turn of speed. I missed third, then found it, and all of a sudden I remembered how to drive a truck.

When we reached the Kennington Road the jeep

was nowhere to be seen and it was beginning to get dark. The traffic was chocka heading south so I took a chance and turned towards the river and let the heavy vehicle have its head. We roared down towards the War Museum with the empty skip swaying from side to side behind us and banging on the hoists.

As we came up to the lights Fiona shouted, 'Turn right, turn right, they're there!'

I cut across the traffic, narrowly missing a Porsche, and saw the jeep up ahead, the remains of its canvas top flapping in the breeze. It turned towards Blackfriars and left again towards the river at the bottom of the Waterloo Road.

'Be careful,' said Fiona over the roar of the truck's engine. 'If he sees us, he'll shoot.'

'No more shells for the shotgun,' I replied. 'Two at the restaurant. Three more to take out the BMW.'

'He might have another gun.'

'Use this then.' And I tossed her the revolver. She checked the cylinder. What a woman.

Teddy was observing the speed limit but I wasn't. I caught him as we came up to Waterloo Station and bumped him so hard that the jeep shivered from the impact. Lupus looked back through the hole in the soft top and shouted something to him. Up ahead, blue lights flashed at the Bull Ring roundabout at Waterloo Bridge, and I knew they were captured and so did they. Oh no, boys, I thought. You're not going to get away that easy. I have a long memory and they'd been taking the piss too long. I could smell revenge in my nostrils like burning flesh.

I looked through the wide windscreen of the truck and had an idea. The Bull Ring is a big concrete hole in the ground, fifteen or twenty feet below the road level. Some town and country planner in the dim and distant must have thought that a circular concrete walkway, surrounded on all sides by one of the busiest intersections south of the river, with a dozen or more tunnels entering and leaving it, would be the ideal spot for a refreshing coffee and croissant break. So they dotted the place with a few iron seats and put some murals on the walls and forgot about it. What it turned into was an unhealthy bunker for cardboard city where the dossers could drink themselves stupid and breathe carbon monoxide at all hours of the day and night. The place stank of shit and piss, and packs of half-crazed dogs roamed through the tunnels. It was like a Hogarthian theme park knee deep in garbage. The big hole yawned open to the sky, surrounded by a four foot high wall of stressed concrete stained yellow by the weather and the constant car emissions.

Teddy slowed, but I wasn't having any and caught the back of the jeep with the big front bumper of the truck as we came out on to the roundabout. Teddy tried to pull away but the jeep was all tangled up with the skip lorry and didn't have a tenth of its power. I pushed down on the accelerator, slewed right and slammed the smaller vehicle against the wall around the edge of the Ring. Concrete flew. The metal of the jeep crumpled and its tyres smoked.

'What are you doing?' screamed Fiona.

'They were going to kill us,' I said through gritted

teeth, but I didn't know if she could hear me above the racket. 'Now I'm giving them some pay back.'

I dropped down a gear and kept pushing. The wall bulged and collapsed slowly inwards. The jeep went through, tilted for a second, and the bodywork caught the light as it dropped. I heard the sound of the engine revving to a scream as it fell.

The impact was hard and metallic and the engine cut. There was silence for ten seconds or so after it hit, then the gas tank exploded and a ball of greasy red smoke mushroomed out of the hole in the ground. I switched off the engine of the truck and slumped over the wheel, reaching for Fiona's hand. She squeezed my fingers and I squeezed back.

After a few seconds I rolled up the side window because I knew exactly what the smoke would smell like.

29

I saw Emerald one more time. I was back in hospital,
but a prison hospital this time. Brixton. My leg was in
plaster again, and in traction. I'd fucked it up good
and proper driving that truck. By the time I got out I
figured I'd be due for a disability pension. The place
wasn't too bad. The food was crap but I was on my
own and it was warm. I had a permanent guard too.
He brought me in chocolate and cigarettes.

Emerald came one afternoon early in the
new year. He looked older and smaller than I
remembered.

'Nicky,' he said as he pulled up a chair to the bedside. The officer stood and looked out through the
bars of the window over Jebb Avenue.

'Emerald,' I replied. 'How are you?'

'Better than you by the looks of it.'

'That wouldn't be difficult, at least you're out.'

'Thanks to you I am, and so will you be. I've got the
best brief in town working on it.'

'Bail? I don't think so,' I said. 'I've done this once
too often. I think I'm in for good.'

'For an accident that happened while they were
trying to kill you? Your foot slipped off the clutch so
I heard. Too bad.'

'Too bad,' I agreed.

'You've done me a good turn, Nicky. I won't

forget that. I've made sure your bank balance is looking better.'

'Thanks, Em. So what else is new?'

'I'm retiring, Nicky.'

'What, you?'

'Yeah. I'm selling my places to Bim, just like he always wanted.'

'I don't believe it.'

'I'm getting old, Nicky. Too old for all this. I didn't know what was going on under my own nose. They stitched me up good and proper. Family too, and someone I thought was a friend. That would never have happened in the old days.'

I didn't argue.

'I've made a lot of money. I'm going home. There's a warm place waiting for me and the missus. Better than this cold bloody country. I always hated the weather here.'

'Sounds good,' I said.

'But I promise you one thing, Nicky. Before I leave you'll be back in circulation. You've got my word on that.'

'Your word was always good enough for me, Em. You know that.'

'You've been a good friend, Nick. Better than my own. I'll never forget it.'

'And I'll never forget you, Em.'

We shook hands. The officer ignored the breach of regulations.

'Keep smiling, Nick. You've got a good woman waiting for you.'

'I know, Em.' He lumbered to his feet and the officer let him out.

He kept his word, but I never saw him again.

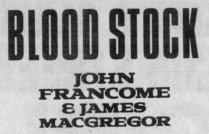

More Thrilling Fiction from Headline:

JOSEPH R. GARBER
RASCAL MONEY

A *Catch-22* for the business world of the nineties

Scott Thatcher devoted his life to building PegaSys Inc. into one of America's biggest – and best – computer companies. Now he's going to lose it all – to the worst-run company in the Western World . . .

RASCAL MONEY

Thatcher's up against a deadline. Whoever is bankrolling his opponents with enough junk bonds to buy IBM is prepared to stoop to anything – murder included – to bring Thatcher down. Worse, PegaSys Inc.'s supposedly infallible systems have been penetrated by the mad hacker Wintergreen, and even Thatcher's tame eccentric genius Knight can't flush him out. *And* Thatcher's high-flying lieutenants, Mike Ash and Louise Bowman, have fallen deeply in lust. Time is running out . . .

RASCAL MONEY

An unputdownable and blackly funny thriller of computers and high finance.

'Fast, funny, outrageous, and a damn good read. He does for capitalism what the Visigoths did for Rome' *San Francisco Chronicle*

FICTION/THRILLER   0 7472 3442 6

A selection of bestsellers
from Headline

FICTION

A WOMAN ALONE	Malcolm Ross	£4.99 ☐
BRED TO WIN	William Kinsolving	£4.99 ☐
MISTRESS OF GREEN TREE MILL	Elisabeth McNeill	£4.50 ☐
SHADES OF FORTUNE	Stephen Birmingham	£4.99 ☐
RETURN OF THE SWALLOW	Frances Anne Bond	£4.99 ☐
THE SERVANTS OF TWILIGHT	Dean R Koontz	£4.99 ☐
WHITE LIES	Christopher Hyde	£4.99 ☐
PEACEMAKER	Robert & Frank Holt	£4.99 ☐

NON-FICTION

FIRST CONTACT	Ben Bova & Byron Preiss (eds)	£5.99 ☐
NEWTON'S MADNESS	Harold L Klawans	£4.99 ☐

SCIENCE FICTION AND FANTASY

HYPERION	Dan Simmons	£4.99 ☐
SHADOW REALM	Marc Alexander	£4.99 ☐
Wells of Ythan 3		

All Headline books are available at your local bookshop or newsagent, or can be ordered direct from the publisher. Just tick the titles you want and fill in the form below. Prices and availability subject to change without notice.

Headline Book Publishing PLC, Cash Sales Department, PO Box 11, Falmouth, Cornwall, TR10 9EN, England.

Please enclose a cheque or postal order to the value of the cover price and allow the following for postage and packing:
UK: 80p for the first book and 20p for each additional book ordered up to a maximum charge of £2.00
BFPO: 80p for the first book and 20p for each additional book
OVERSEAS & EIRE: £1.50 for the first book, £1.00 for the second book and 30p for each subsequent book.

Name ....

Address ....

....

....